A squad of troops was running along the wall above the alcove. Maximov smiled. They would get the invaders! His smile turned into a look of horrified amazement as the squad suddenly pitched and writhed as bullets ripped into them. A short, ugly man in black fatigues ran to the edge and called down to the other invaders. When the black-clad man trained his gun on the wall and fired a long sweeping burst that worked its way toward him, Maximov ducked behind the stones. The bullets whined loudly as they ricocheted off the wall.

There was only one group insane enough to attack him here and tough enough to survive.

"Marauders!" Maximov cursed. Then he smiled. They would not get away from here! They were as trapped as he was, and he had an army to back him up. The Marauders were as good as dead . . .

THE MARAUDERS

FORTRESS
OF DEATH

MICHAEL MCGANN

JOVE BOOKS, NEW YORK

FORTRESS OF DEATH

A Jove Book / published by arrangement with
the author

PRINTING HISTORY
Jove edition / November 1991

ISBN: 0-515-10687-9

Jove Books are published by The Berkley Publishing Group,
200 Madison Avenue, New York, New York 10016.
The name "JOVE" and the "J" logo
are trademarks belonging to Jove Publications, Inc.

10   9   8   7   6   5   4   3   2   1

For Sherry

"I am Shiva,
the destroyer of worlds . . ."

ONE

The long dark hull looked like a huge underwater coffin.

That's what it had been for the 85 Soviet submariners who died in the attack sub after it was detected by a U.S. Navy P-3 Orion early on in the big Nuke-Out. The upright conning tower sat like a tombstone halfway back along the wide oval hull.

The Orion had dropped two MK-50 anti-submarine torpedoes on the nuclear attack sub. The two shaped-charge warheads had penetrated the Sierra's double hulls, blasting the crew with twin jets of fire as hot as the sun, and then putting out the fire with a few hundred tons of ice-cold seawater.

Now the Sierra lay in ninety-five feet of water, nestled into the mud of the Baltic Sea.

Gunter Müeller kicked his way down the hull, moving backward from the conning tower toward the huge tail fin, whose prominent sonar pod loomed in the murky distance. He found the large, round weapons-loading hatch open. Apparently, some of the doomed sailors had tried to escape from the stricken boat to the surface.

Müeller sat for a moment looking down into the dark, murky interior of the sub. The boat was a crypt; a metal coffin filled with rotting sailors, dead now for years. The thought of those drowned sailors chilled him worse than the cold water.

They are dead, Gunter, he reminded himself, but you are not. He turned on his dive light and shined it down into the sub. The inky blackness seemed to absorb the light. Gunter took a deep breath and kicked slowly through the hatch into the black interior of the sub.

Inside, the sub was both remarkably intact and chaotically destroyed. The rushing water had swirled up every moveable object in the sub. Now much of the debris floated overhead. The sub's gear was all still intact—at least here where the fire from the torpedo warheads had not penetrated. Müeller swam past the command center, moving forward now toward his goal: the torpedo room. The sub's flooded interior was silent. His breath, blown out through the scuba regulator's mouthpiece, sounded like thunder in the eerie silence.

Now and then, the weak beam from his light picked up an arm or a leg hanging down from the mass of debris on the sub's ceiling. The cold water prevented much decay, even in summer, and the bodies of the dead crew floated up with the rest of the garbage. He was tempted to loot the bodies for their rubber-soled canvas shoes, their dead men's jewelry and East German watches, but the thought of their bloated white faces made him sick. Müeller tried to ignore the grisly stalactites.

Beyond the command center, the torpedo control room was a shambles. The torpedo had hit on the starboard side. Its fiery jet had knifed through the torpedo control room like a blowtorch through a cracker box. The machinery here was all melted, twisted and torn. Müeller shined his light down the right wall. The hole in the pressure hull was half a meter wide. Müeller didn't want to contemplate what it had been like in this room.

Poor bastards, he thought as he mentally traced the path of the fire. It must have felt like a dozen flamethrowers followed by a sledgehammer.

Müeller shook off the grisly thought and swam down the ladder to the torpedo room. His light seemed unable to pierce the thick gloom. He found scorch marks on the paint and metal fixtures near the ladder. The fire from above must have come in here, too. Further forward, there were no scorch marks. The fire had not gotten to the weapons!

On the lower racks behind the 533mm torpedo tubes, he found the prize he had come for. Nestled in their shipping containers were the two remaining SS-NX-21 cruise missiles! Although he could not read Russian, he could make out the weapon designation and the radioactive warning symbols on the containers. The two missiles had nuclear warheads!

Müeller shouted through his mouthpiece, the garbled sound disappearing into the deadly silence.

The chairman will pay dearly for these! He laughed as he swam back toward the ladder. I will be a rich man!

He glanced at the makeshift dive watch on his wrist. He had been down here too long. He would have to wait under the surface a few minutes to decompress so he would not get the bends. Ordinarily, he would hate the wait in the frigid water, but today, it would be no problem. He could wait a few minutes to be rich. Ten meters below the surface, he held onto his boat's anchor line, dreaming about his forthcoming riches as he waited out the minutes.

When he finally struggled back into his skiff, his lips were blue and he was shaking all over. A deep swallow from the bottle of cheap schnapps warmed him enough to start the old outboard motor.

As he turned the skiff back toward Rostov, Müeller laughed. He had been in this very skiff when the Orion had flown over, dropping sonar buoys and circling. He had watched the two torpedoes fall from the plane, their tiny parachutes streaming out behind to point them nose down at the steel-grey water. He had heard the thunderous booms underwater and felt the salt spray from the geysers of water thrown up by the explosions.

In the chaos that followed the war, he had forgotten the submarine. He had remembered it last month while listening to two old sailors swap lies over a liter of potato beer. It had taken him a month to find the scuba gear to make the dive. It had been easy to find the sub. It was just where the American Navy had left it.

Everyone knew that Maximov wanted nuclear weapons to use against the Free Nations. He would reward Müeller well for these two, maybe even give him a job in the FSE's rag-tag navy.

"The trick now," he said to the sullen charcoal-grey clouds that merged with the dark water to form a wall of gloom, "is to find a way to reach Maximov without some flunky stealing the reward!" That would take some thought, but he would find a way. Even the cold wind that blew across the grey water could not affect Müeller's elation. He killed the bottle of schnapps on the way back.

On the shore, the two men watched Müeller tie up his boat to the rotting pier and pedal away on his bicycle, whistling.

"So," the taller of the two said softly, "he has found it."

"Apparently," his companion agreed, stowing the large binoculars in his shoulder bag.

"How long do you think it will take them to salvage the boat?" the tall man asked as he rolled over on his back and sat up against the bush that had hidden them from Müeller. He lit a short stub of a cigarette.

"Not long, I expect," his companion replied. "The chairman will want the missiles as soon as possible. I doubt that they will wait until spring to start bringing them up."

"Should we alert the other side now?" the tall man asked, pulling the smoke deep into his lungs.

"No," the shorter man said, taking the cigarette from his friend for one puff, "we should make sure that the FSE can really bring them up first. If they cannot, there is no need to alarm everyone."

The other man nodded, drew one last drag from his smoke, then snubbed it out and put the butt in his pocket. "It seems so long since the Riga went down."

"I know," his friend answered. "It was during our previous life!"

The tall man chuckled. "Before the world went to hell."

"Uumm," the shorter one agreed. "Still, we have full bellies and no one's boot on our necks. We live well, compared with most people in Europe!" The two sat silent for a moment. "We could still be on the Riga with Yuri and the others." His friend nodded and hooked his thumb toward the tree line. The two men slipped down the small hill and disappeared into the trees.

"OOWWWW! Jesus!" Jack Keenan screamed, clutching at his face with both hands. "You're tryin' to kill me! What kind of fuckin' vacation is this anyhow?"

"I'm sorry Jack," Dr. Saltman apologized, "we need a photo for your file. You may be the only person who has survived Rilchinski's gas. As such, you are a very valuable person to us. You may have the key to an antidote in your blood."

"So for that you have to set off an A-bomb in my face?" Keenan growled.

Saltman smiled. "A flashbulb is hardly an A-bomb, Jack."

"Not to *my* jumped-up eyeballs, it isn't!" Keenan snapped, lurching up out of the chair and pacing back and forth in front of the large windows that made up one side of the narrow lab. "And another thing, how many more little tortures am I going to have to endure? You've poked me, pinched me, whispered at me, made me smell a bunch of weird shit; put, God-knows-what, in my mouth to taste; you've done everything but jack me off!"

"We're going to do that today!" Saltman answered brightly. Keenan whirled around, his face covered with a dark scowl. "Just kidding, Jack," Saltman said quickly, holding both hands up in front of him, palms out.

"Well, I wouldn't put it past you!" Keenan flopped back down in the metal folding chair. "Tell you the truth," he went on, the anger fading from his voice, "I'm about half afraid to masturbate. Everything else is so intense, I'm afraid I couldn't handle a hand-job, much less a piece of ass."

Saltman looked intently at the huge nervous man seated before him. Crazy Jack Keenan was a legend, an almost mythical creature. He and his comrades, the Marauders, had fought the dark forces of the FSE for years, fighting against overwhelming odds. Now he was engaged in another war, a war within himself.

Keenan had inhaled the neurotoxin developed by Dr. Rilchinski, a renegade FSE scientist. The toxin worked on the sensory areas of the brain, heightening each sensation to the threshold of pain. The victims usually went mad from the sensory overload, then ripped themselves and everything around them to bits.

Keenan had survived his exposure. Now he had superhuman sensory abilities. He could hear whispers hundreds-of-yards away, and see in total darkness. He could sense danger at a distance, too; something that could not be explained by simple sensory enhancement.

But although he was a fascinating research subject, he was also a warrior. He detested being poked and stared at. Saltman knew he needed to give Keenan a break or he would lose him altogether.

"Listen, Jack," he suggested, "why don't you take a break for a few days. We've pushed you pretty hard, why don't you take a week off and just unwind?"

"Damn straight!" Keenan thundered, suddenly much happier, "I'll be back here next Monday. You can jack me off then." He jumped up from the chair and started for the door, then turned and leered over his shoulder. "That is if there's anything left to jack off!" He roared with laughter as he pushed through the double doors and disappeared into the hall.

Saltman took off his round, wire rimmed glasses and studiously cleaned them on his lab coat. This done, he turned to the windows and watched Jack Keenan sprint down the sidewalk that led to his room in the staff quarters.

"Come back, Jack," Saltman said softly. "Come back, we need you!"

"Easy, Pete," Freddie Mamudi murmured as the whisker-thin line jumped and twitched, "let him swallow the whole thing!"

"I got him," Kinski answered, his hand sliding slowly up the fiberglass rod, "I got him."

"Now!" Mamudi barked.

Kinski jerked hard on the rod. Immediately, the reel began to whine as hundreds of feet of monofilament line raced out through the ferrules.

"Let him run 'til he stops, then start working him back in," Mamudi said smiling, his one eye twinkling. "You'll have a fight on your hands!"

"A fight is what we need," a deep voice growled from behind the two fishermen. "Not this boring vacation crap!"

"Chill out, Buddha!" Kinski called as he watched his line singing out into the cold blue water of the loch. "At least this fish can't kill us!"

"Except maybe with boredom!" Winston S. "Buddha" Chan grumbled. He opened the cabin door and went down into the big cabin cruiser looking for more beer.

On deck, Kinski was struggling with the fish, straining against the rod as he slowly winched in the leviathan. Behind him, Mamudi offered encouragement and frequent swigs of McEwan's Export beer.

Kinski was still struggling ten minutes later when Buddha Chan came back on deck.

"Aren't you through yet?" Chan growled.

"Just getting to the hard part!" Mamudi exclaimed. "When the fish is near the boat, you can lose him easy!"

"Yeah?" Chan asked, "maybe I can help you there!" He disappeared back below decks. Intent on their catch, Kinski and Mamudi ignored their bored friend. They didn't notice when he came back on deck carrying a long nylon case.

One hundred meters out, the big pike was fighting hard, leaping out of the water, shaking its head to dislodge the big hook.

"Watch him!" Mamudi shouted as the big fish broke the surface in a huge leap. "He'll throw it!"

Kinski didn't have time to answer. Behind them, the roar of Chan's M14 rifle boomed out over the water.

"Damn it, Chan," Kinski screamed, twisting his head around, "what the hell are you tryin' to do? Blow my head off?"

"No," Chan answered, his face split by a demonic smile, "I just wanted to make sure your fish didn't get away!"

Kinski and Mamudi both turned to look at the line. It was slack, tangling on the deck like blue glass noodles.

"See what you did?" Mamudi said darkly,. "You have caused Peter to lose the fish after all that work."

"Au contraire, mes amis," Chan retorted, bringing the scope down from his eye, "reel it in."

Kinski began to reel in the loose line. In a moment, the line became taut again, but there was no struggle. Two minutes later, the pike came to the surface. Kinski hauled it up as Mamudi hooked it with the gaff. The fish was quite dead. There was a large hole just behind the left eye, and a much larger hole on the other side.

"I don't believe it!" Kinski gasped. "A head shot on my fish!"

"You're too kind," Chan answered as he removed the magazine from his rifle and jacked the round out of the chamber.

"Kind, my ass!" Kinski wailed. "You ruined it! The whole point is to fight it all the way to the boat—not zap it with heavy artillery!" Kinski slumped in his chair. Mamudi pulled the big hook from the pike's mouth and hooked it onto Kinski's reel, taking up the slack on the line.

"If you didn't want to come fishing," he asked Chan, "why did you come?"

"Because it's better than being holed up in a hotel room or pawed at by every passerby on the sidewalk." He put the rifle back in its case and slumped down against the bulkhead. "Since we got back, everyone treats us like we're the fuckin' royal family. I'm just a Gyrene. I'm not used to being treated like some kind of celebrity." He frowned as Mamudi handed him a beer. "Another thing, I hate this damn English beer!"

Mamudi smiled, "It's Scotch beer."

"Whatever," Chan growled, taking a huge swig, "I hate it." He looked down the length of the loch. A storm was building in the north. "I wonder if they've dissected poor Jack yet?"

As Kinski stuffed his catch into the boat's big ice chest, Mamudi started the engine and turned the boat back toward the hotel dock. The three soldiers rode back in silence, each lost in his own concern for their leader.

TWO

Yevgeny Maximov stared out at the steel-grey clouds that hung low over Hamburg. The dark clouds formed a background of gloom for the City of Despair.

His headquarters here was a monolith of concrete and steel on the edge of an industrial park. Hamburg had escaped the nuclear fires that had consumed many German cities during the war. There seemed to be no reason for Hamburg's luck, but during the madness of war, most things happened for no reason.

Maximov was waiting to hear from Ernst Kruger, his most recent chief of staff. After the debacle in Spain, he had replaced many of his previous staff. Their successors were painfully aware of the seriousness of their promotions. Several of the newly appointed officers had the honor of shooting their former bosses. Kruger was one of these.

The intercom's raucous squawk startled him, even though he was waiting for it.

"Yes?" he barked.

"Comrade Chairman," Kruger's voice crackled through the speaker, his heavy Prussian accent easily recognizable, "I have Herr Müeller with me. His claim seems authentic."

"Bring him in," Maximov snapped, terminating the conversation. He looked back out the window. The dark clouds were dropping a torrential rain on Hamburg.

"If you are lying, Müeller," he said to the plate glass, "I

9

will make your skin into a lamp shade." He was almost afraid to get excited over the man's message. Müeller claimed to have two nuclear weapons! His letter had said no more than that, but now Kruger seemed to believe him, too. Kruger was no gullible fool. If Müeller had been lying, he would be dead by now.

The carved door opened and Kruger walked in, followed by a tall, thin man who walked unsteadily. Müeller had the weathered face of a man who works on the sea, a fisherman or a merchant sailor. His dark leathery skin contrasted with his nearly white hair and pale blue eyes. The dark skin did little to conceal the even darker bruises on his cheeks and forehead. His upper lip was split and puffy. Kruger had obviously interrogated the man using the rubber truncheon he referred to as his "lie detector." The two men stood behind the plush chairs that faced his polished desk. He motioned them to sit, but stood looking out the window, watching the storm.

"So, Herr Müeller," Maximov said quietly, turning his head toward the battered visitor, "you have something for me?"

"Yes, Chairman Maximov!" Müeller replied, his speech a bit slurred by the cut lip, "I have two guided missiles with nuclear warheads!"

Maximov stepped over to the throne-like leather chair which stood behind his desk and leaned on it, his arms crossed. "That is exciting news." He arched his eyebrows. "Where did you find these missiles?"

"In a Russian submarine, Chairman Maximov," Müeller stammered, "a sunken submarine. They are cruise missiles."

"How do you know so much about Soviet missiles, Herr Müeller," Maximov asked as he pulled the chair back and sat in it, leaning back.

"I watched the submarine fire the others," Müeller answered, "during the war. I saw an American plane attack the submarine."

Maximov cast his eyes at Kruger, seeking affirmation. Kruger was quick to answer. "His description of the launches is consistent with cruise missile launches from a submerged submarine, sir," Kruger explained, "he has described the general outline of a Soviet Sierra class sub, one of the types of Soviet submarines capable of launching such missiles." Kruger smiled wolfishly at Müeller. "I am convinced he is telling the truth."

Maximov looked back at Müeller. The man's gaze was steady, not pleading or shifty. Maximov took a moment to reflect on his course of action. He could have Kruger torture the missiles' location out of the man, but Müeller looked like the sort who might die before he cracked. That would cost him his greatest desire, nuclear weapons. No, it would be better this time to buy the man instead. He clearly wanted something for the information. It would be a lot simpler just to give it to him.

"What is it that you wish in return for these missiles?"

Müeller sat up in his chair and looked the chairman in the eye. "I wish a cash reward," he said calmly, "and to serve as a commissioned officer in your navy."

"How large a cash reward?" Maximov asked.

Müeller was silent for a second, then said firmly, "I will let you place a value on the weapons when you have seen them."

Maximov turned his chair toward the window for a second so Müeller could not see his face.

What an idiot! he thought. He could ask for half of Europe and get it, and all he wants is a reward and a commission. A warm flood of excitement washed over Maximov. This fool would be his ticket to absolute power. Maximov turned his chair back around. He smiled broadly at Müeller, then stood and reached across the desk, his hand extended.

"Congratulations, Herr Müeller," Maximov beamed. "You have done well to bring these missiles to me. Such loyalty and devotion must be rewarded!"

Müeller stood and shook the Chairman's hand. "Danke," he gushed, "danke schoen, Chairman Maximov!"

Maximov turned to Kruger. "Ernst, see to it that our guest has an apartment and get him some suitable clothes. See to it that he has plenty to eat and drink and that he is entertained." Kruger nodded.

"Herr Müeller," Maximov went on, "you shall be amply rewarded, I assure you! Tomorrow, we will commission you as a commander in the FSE Navy. Then you can organize the salvage of the missiles."

Müeller leapt to his feet and stood at attention. "Yes, sir," he snapped, causing the split in his lip to open up and bleed again, "Thank you again, Chairman Maximov!"

"It is I who thank you, Comrade," Maximov crooned, walking around the desk to escort Müeller toward the door, "we will speak again tomorrow." At the door, Kruger took Müeller in tow and the two men left.

Back at his desk, Maximov stared back out at the brooding clouds. Soon there would be a cloud over London, an atomic cloud. Soon King Shatterhand would taste Maximov's nuclear fire.

A sudden dark thought crossed Maximov's mind. The Marauders. They had thwarted his plans in the past; they must not be permitted to interfere with this plan.

Maximov sat back down at his desk, his mood becoming as dark as the lowering clouds outside. Those four bastards had been a knife in his side for years! He knew from his spy that they were still in England, but he could not count on them staying there.

What I need is for them to be occupied for a few weeks while I get my nuclear arsenal up and running, he mused; something that they could not drop.

A cruel smile crept across his face. The one thing that would keep them in England was an attempt on the new king's life. No, several attempts! They would never leave if the king was in danger!

Maximov laughed out loud. If they were close to the king when the first nuclear cruise missile went off over them, he would be rid of the lot of them at once! That thought cheered Maximov immensely.

He would put Butakov on this mission. Butakov hated the Marauders. He would keep them busy. He might even kill the king before the nuke arrived! Either way, Maximov would be the winner.

He looked back out the window as a thunderclap shook the building and rain pelted against the glass.

What a wonderful day! he thought.

THREE

The last two weeks had been a blur. Müeller felt like a god. Maximov had been as good as his word. Müeller was now a commander in the FSE Navy with a salvage barge and a crew that followed his orders. It was a far cry from his days as a poor fisherman! The barge was old and its crane was small, but it was his and in a few days, he would be rich.

Now, as he sat in his room looking down on his barge tied to the wharf below, he was filled with pride. The FSE had taken over the entire hotel, much to the displeasure of the owner and his family. The FSE was not in the habit of paying for lodging, and the owner's attractive young wife had drawn some lustful stares from the divers and security troops. She had disappeared the next day. Her husband claimed that she had gone to see her sister. That was just as well, she would have been a distraction to their mission here. Müeller wanted to get the missiles up to the surface as soon as possible.

Maximov had put off the matter of the reward until the missiles were recovered, saying that he did not pay for goods until they were delivered. That made sense. Müeller never paid for anything until it was in his hand, either. He was not worried. Maximov had done everything he had promised, so far. He would pay for these missiles, too.

In the street below, the divers and barge crewmen emerged from the hotel. Müeller slugged back the last of the wretched coffee substitute and was reaching for his jacket when the knock came at his door.

"Commander Müeller," Ernst Kruger's voice boomed through the door, "The men are ready!"

"Coming!" Müeller replied, slipping on the Blue FSE jacket. In spite of their unpleasant first meeting, Müeller liked Kruger. He was a no-nonsense leader who inspired, if not loyalty, at least fear in his subordinates. Müeller liked that, and wanted to be like that, too.

Twenty minutes later, the Ariel cast off and began her slow trip up the coast to the tiny bay Müeller knew so well.

Ernst Kruger watched the gray water curl back from the Ariel's bow. The old tub was slow and the trip would take most of the day. Kruger did not like the water and looked forward to finishing this little job. His orders were simple. Get the missiles, then come back. Whatever else he did was his business.

Müeller figured it would take four days to get the missiles up from the sunken sub. Kruger doubted it would go that fast. Something always happened. Either the weather turned bad or somebody got hurt. They would be here at least a week. Too bad that luscious piece at the hotel had disappeared. Oh well.

The Ariel rode over a swell that made Kruger's stomach lurch. This would be a long day.

Hours later, Müeller's excited cry signalled the end of the wallowing ride.

"There," Müeller shouted from the Ariel's tiny bridge, "see the white marker?"

Kruger shaded his eyes with his hand and slowly scanned the dark water. A tiny white speck appeared several hundred meters away, then disappeared in the swells. The Ariel made for the little marker. They would anchor right above the wreck.

Even before the barge stopped, the divers were on deck, pulling on their rubber suits and scuba gear. As soon as the engine stopped, they splashed over the side and disappeared into the murky water. In minutes they were up again, giving anchoring directions to the barge crew.

By the time the Ariel was anchored above the sunken Sierra, the sun was low in the sky. Leaving a squad of guards on board for the night, the salvage party took the launch back to the hotel.

Kruger listened with barely concealed annoyance as Müeller nattered on about finding the wreck. He had heard the story a dozen times already. It was the same one he had beat out of Müeller in the first place. The memory of Müeller's interrogation picked up Kruger's spirits a bit.

Two weeks ago, I beat the hell out of him, Kruger smiled to himself as Müeller rambled on, and now we are best friends. What a fool!

It was dark when they finally tied up at the small pier. Müeller insisted on a small party to celebrate. He and the divers commandeered the tiny bar in the hotel to toast the project. The bar was empty except for two big men men who sat at a small table in the back. They were talking quietly to themselves, but something about them made Kruger uneasy. They had that dangerous look, somehow. As the crew filled the bar, the two men paid and left. Kruger made a mental note to watch for them again.

At midnight, Kruger shut down the party. They had to leave just after sunup to get to the site by mid morning. The divers would be hung over enough as it was.

"What a wet blanket!" Müeller grumbled as he pulled off his uniform shirt and tossed it on the shabby little dresser in his room. "The party was just getting rolling. Oh, well. Tomorrow the real fun begins!"

The thought of bringing up the two missiles made him laugh out loud. After his reward, he would throw a real party!

As he stepped over to the wash basin, Müeller noticed the flare of a match in the darkness out on the wharf. He peered into the blackness. Two men were walking slowly up the pier.

Odd that they were out so late, he thought as he splashed the cold water on his face. He would mention it to Kruger in the morning. Müeller crawled between the thin sheets and pulled the blanket up. He dozed off thinking about the party he would throw when he was rich.

Victor T'sinko took one last drag on the harsh cigarette and snubbed it out beneath his boot.

"How long will it take them?" his companion Arkady Kron asked, as he straddled the small motorbike and kicked the little engine to life.

"They will probably have the first one up day after tomorrow," T'sinko answered, sitting behind Kron on the bike's long seat. "In a week, they will have them all."

Kron nodded in reply and twisted the hand grip. The little bike puttered off, leaving the dark port town behind them. The two big men looked absurd on the small bike, but there was no one to notice.

Thirty minutes later, Kron turned the bike up a narrow, nearly invisible path off the paved road. T'sinko stepped off the back of the bike and carefully hid the tire track until there was no trace of their turn-off. The tall trees muffled the sound of the tiny engine as it disappeared deeper into the forest.

FOUR

Ivan Butakov popped the lens covers off the binoculars and slowly searched the rocky beach five hundred meters ahead for any sign of life. The beach seemed empty, devoid of any life except the few seagulls that wheeled overhead, their harsh cries muffled by the thick mist.

It was a perfect morning for infiltration, clear enough to see the objective, but too overcast to be picked up by some flying observer.

Butakov knew the area. He had been here twice before, inserting a spy two years ago, and again, eleven months ago, to insert the first spy's replacement.

It was a typical English beach. There was no sand, only pebbles. On either side of the beach, sharp outcroppings waited to snare the incautious traveler and dash him to bits on the huge boulders. The outcroppings also served to hide the beach from view on either side, a definite advantage.

Butakov looked over his shoulder at the other two inflatable boats following closely in his wake. Like his, each boat held five men. The teams were hand picked. Each man was a ruthless killer with no regard for his own safety. Butakov was reasonably certain that each of the fifteen men were capable of doing the job alone. In three packs of five, they would surely kill the new king.

He looked at the blackened faces of the men in his team. Shakevich was a certified psychotic. He believed that the

English had started the war and pulled the Americans and the Soviets into it. He hated all Englishmen. Schmitt was a professional killer before the war, working for the gangsters in Hamburg as an assassin. He killed for money, although Butakov suspected he would do it as well for the pure enjoyment. Flanagan was an IRA survivor who had come to Maximov after the problem in Ireland. He would shoot a man for wearing English Leather cologne. Harley was a Brit himself. He had been a policeman once, in Manchester. He blamed the war and the destruction on the old government. The fact that the old government was destroyed now, was irrelevant to him. Regicide was his only goal now.

There's never been a worse collection of scum and villainy than the men in this boat, he thought grimly, except, perhaps, for the men in the other two boats.

The landing was uneventful and unchallenged. After deflating the boats and storing them in the rocks, the three teams set off toward their respective hiding spots.

Spartacus, the spy he had brought ashore here eleven months ago, had set up several hiding places and three safe houses for the teams to stay in once they were ashore.

The other two teams set off on foot, waiting an hour between departure to avoid being spotted all together. Butakov's team stayed near the beach, watching the deserted road from a spot in the rocks. The spy would pick him and the other four men up, and take them to London.

Once there, they would map out a plan to kill the king.

Two hours passed without any sign of the man. The sun was trying hard to burn through the thick clouds, but having little luck. Finally, the sound of an engine whined in the stillness.

Spartacus drove up in an old Land Rover, stopped, got out and stretched, then turned and relieved himself on the tire of the rugged vehicle. He was rezipping his pants when Butakov and the others walked up behind him.

"Where the fuck have you been?" Butakov snarled. "We could have been spotted!"

"Waiting long?" the spy asked, as the four others climbed into the back of the Rover.

"Too long!" snapped Butakov.

"Sorry," the spy smiled, "shall we go then?"

He climbed behind the wheel as Butakov got in, started the Rover, made a quick U-turn, and sped off toward London.

"A familiar spot, that, eh?" Spartacus asked, tilting his head back toward the isolated beach. The man looked very different now, than he had that night, so many months ago.

His sandy blond hair was carefully coiffed now, his pale skin scrubbed clean. He wore a tweed jacket and green canvas pleated pants with tall, brown leather boots that gleamed. A vast change from the scared little man he had almost had to throw onto the beach back then. Now he seemed confident and self assured.

What a little fop, Butakov thought, what a pitiful spy!

Still, Spartacus was alive, and that was more than could be said for his predecessor. They drove the three hours to the safe house in silence. Once at the safe house, Spartacus's part in their mission would be over.

They were half an hour away from their destination when they ran into the roadblock. It was set up at a bend in the road. Six soldiers and two policemen manned it. They seemed to be checking vehicle documents.

"Stay calm," Spartacus hissed, "let me do the talking."

Butakov knew that they would be safer if they kept a low profile, but he also knew the men in the back were not capable of such subtlety. He slid the heavy Makarov pistol out of his belt and hid it up the loose sleeve of his jacket. Out of the corner of his eye, he could see the four men in the back moving about, getting their weapons ready.

Spartacus was all smiles when the policeman leaned down to his window. "May I see your license and registration, Sir?" the policeman asked.

"Surely," Spartacus replied. "What seems to be the problem?"

"Just a routine check," the copper answered, reaching for the papers.

Butakov swung the pistol up in front of Spartacus's face and fired. The little spy's scream filled the space between the two shots. The policeman's head snapped back twice, then he fell forward, leaving a red trail down the Rover's door.

The men in the back were not idle. As the soldiers and the remaining policeman reached for their weapons, the four assassins cut them down with quick bursts from their mini-Uzis. A grand mal seizure of lead sent each of the hapless soldiers spinning and twitching to the ground.

In four seconds, it was all over. Butakov opened his door and walked around the car. He pulled the policeman off the car door, then methodically shot each of the other victims in the head. This done, he and the other killers dragged the lifeless bodies into the bushes that bordered the road.

"You nearly blew my bloody head off!" Spartacus snapped, as Butakov and the others emerged from the brush after hiding their grisly work. The man's voice had a whining quality to it that set Butakov's teeth on edge.

"You should have leaned back!" Butakov chuckled as he walked up to the car. Spartacus leaned out and looked at the gory red stain that ran down the door.

"Now we'll have to clean that off!" he whined. Butakov stepped back and unzipped his pants.

"I'll take care of it," he said brightly, then began to urinate onto the bloody door. Spartacus quickly rolled up the window to avoid any splatters. The other assassins climbed in the back of the Rover as Butakov finished relieving himself.

"There," Butakov sighed, "fresh as a daisy!" The four others laughed as Butakov climbed back in. Spartacus drove away in silence, fuming.

The mist had burned off by the time they reached the small, secluded house on the edge of London. It was well hidden by a screen of trees. Spartacus dropped them off with a curt, "good luck."

Inside the house, the five men made themselves comfortable, changing into the clothes that Spartacus had provided. They would wait for his call to move.

"Oh, ride me, Eric!" she moaned, "ride me big!"

"Damn it!" Keenan swore, "they're at it again."

The honeymooners downstairs, Eric and Daphne, were making love, something they did every two or three hours all day, and all night long. The downside of Keenan's heightened senses was that he could hear everything, whether he wanted to, or not. He could block out a lot of it, but it was hard to block out a pretty woman moaning passionately and calling out to her lover.

"Ride this big, Eric," Keenan snarled, extending his middle finger toward the floor.

Keenan rolled out of bed and opened the thin shutters. It was a beautiful day outside. The sun lit the wet trees, turning them into hundreds of crystal chandeliers. The little hotel was perched on the side of a hill overlooking a narrow valley. He had come here for solitude, seeking to escape the torrent of physical input at the hospital.

"Lighten up, Jack," Keenan advised himself, "you're just jealous!" He was jealous. A sudden memory washed over him, a memory of another beautiful morning in a place far away. The trees had glistened with ice that morning as Keenan and his wife made love for hours, stopping only to eat the dark bread and cheese they had bought the day before. They had washed it down with champagne.

Hot tears pooled up in his eyes. He crammed his fists into them to drive the tears away. She was gone now, the little resort near Colorado Springs was gone, too. Both had been swept away by the nuclear fire. Jack forced the memories from his mind.

"I gotta get back to work," he muttered, "I really need to shoot some asshole!" He turned from the window and grabbed his ditty bag from under the bed. A floor below, the metal headboard began to slam against the wall. Daphne's cries were muffled by her pillow.

"Fuck the hospital," Keenan spat. "I'm pulling the plug on their experiments!" He stuffed the bag with his clothes. "I'm goin' to find the other guys and go kick some ass! There has to be somebody in the FSE that needs killin'!"

As he paid his bill and stomped out of the hotel, he could hear Eric and his bride finishing their big ride. Keenan threw his bag into the little sportster and wedged his large body behind the wheel. He kicked the engine to life, and sped off toward London, trailing a wisp of blue smoke.

Buddha Chan burst into the room, beaming.

"Drop your cocks and grab your socks!" he roared. "We're back in business!"

"These are my socks," Mamudi said, holding up two long olive drab garments which seemed to be made of woven moss, "My cock is longer, but not quite so green."

"Not quite is right!" Kinski laughed, "what's up, Buddha?"

"Don't know for sure, and don't care," the short square Mongol replied, "All I know is that the King wants us back in London pronto!" He waved the flimsy telegram. Kinski stepped over to take it as Chan began to throw his clothes into the old Alice pack he used as luggage.

"I wonder if this means Jack, too?" Kinski questioned.

The other two Marauders looked at him. Their expressions said that they were concerned about the same thing. All three shared the same secret fear—that Jack Keenan was no longer one of them.

Chan went back to his packing. Mamudi popped out the glass eye with the nautical flag on it and swapped it for one that had a normal bright blue pupil on it. "Of course it does," he said as he inserted the glass globe into the socket. He looked up at Kinski, who laughed.

"You look just like an Australian sheepdog!" Kinski observed.

"Of course," Mamudi agreed, "I have to herd you two sheep along!" The lithe Afghan laughed as he, too, gathered up his few belongings for the trip back to London.

"This was not the work of criminals," Keenan observed as he looked through the small pile of photos. "Whoever did this knew how to kill quickly and efficiently."

He passed the photos to the other three Marauders. They winced as they looked at the glossies.

"We believe they are in or near London now," Inspector Callahan explained. "We don't know what they are up to, but we want to be safe; not sorry."

"You want us to track them down and dust 'em?" Kinski asked. Chan eagerly nodded in agreement. Mamudi fingered the zipper-like scar on his face.

"Not really," the Scotland Yard inspector answered, "we are more concerned about the safety of the King."

Keenan nodded. The killings had FSE written all over them. The only target worth the effort to send assassins to England was the King.

"We have arranged for the King to go to the hunting lodge at Balmoral," Callahan went on. "We feel this to be the safest place for him for now." The inspector took out a small pipe and chewed on the stem. "It is isolated and the ground around it is open. It should be easy to protect him there."

"To do so will also cause the enemy to come to us," Mamudi agreed. "He will fight where we decide."

"Except he will get to pick when," Keenan observed.

"That's true," Callahan nodded, "but we suspect they will not wait long to attack. The risk of exposure is too great." He filled the pipe from a small sack of tobacco, a precious commodity in post-nuke England. "Of course, we want the four of you to protect him."

The four Americans nodded.

The announcement of the King's hunting trip to Balmoral Castle had caused Spartacus major heartburn, but Butakov had taken it in stride. Shatterhand would be taking a special train from Victoria Station. Butakov had already sent B-team to the station to steal uniforms from the railroad workers.

The basic plan was simple. Shostakovic would start the diversion. When everyone's attention was on him, the other four would attack the King's railway car and kill him. Shatterhand was scheduled to leave at 2300. His men would be in place by 2100.

The small motorcade pulled up in front of Victoria Station right on time. A pair of Special Branch officers led the way. The King, in a heavy Burberry coat and a snap brim hat that almost hid his face, followed them. They went immediately to the King's private train and entered the lounge car.

A minute later, Shostakovic shambled in, his beggar's rags flapping in the cold breeze. He shuffled across the open terminal, accosting the people in the station and generally making a nuisance of himself to draw everyone's attention to him.

He lumbered up to one prosperous couple, grabbing the man's collar.

" 'Ere, Gov," he slurred, breathing a cloud of alcohol fumes in the man's face, "How's about a fiver, eh?"

"Get away!" the man shouted, pushing Shostakovic away. He grabbed his wife's arm and propelled her away from the smelly apparition.

"Thanks, Sport!" Shostakovic hollered, "fuck 'er, I did!"

These antics finally drew the attention of the two uniformed policemen who had been standing at the door of the King's car. They hustled over to take the drunken bum in hand. As they approached, Shostakovic pulled a cigarette and a match from his sleeve and made an exaggerated show of lighting the smoke. The two coppers were nearly upon him when he touched the burning match to his coat.

The coat, soaked in naptha, burst into flame.

"YYYAAAHHH!" Shostakovic screamed as he spun around, slipping the burning coat off his arms. "I'm burning! Get it off me!" He came out of the spin and tossed the burning coat onto the nearest copper.

Now it was the copper's turn to scream as the flaming coat covered him. He flailed at the burning garment. His partner forgot about the drunk for a moment and turned to help his friend. When his eyes left Shostakovic, the suddenly sober drunk pulled a Spanish 9mm pistol from his belt and shot both of the policemen dead.

"Jesus," Kinski swore, "this coat is hot! Does the king really wear this?"

"It is practically his trademark," Mamudi answered, helping Kinski off with the coat. Tacked into the lining of the heavy Burberry were two MP5K submachine guns and Chan's disassembled M14 rifle. Kinski and Mamudi checked the small sub-guns as Chan quickly fitted the action to the stock and snapped the trigger group up. Kinski looked over as Chan pulled the custom silencer up out of his pants.

"And here I thought you were just glad to see me!" he chuckled.

Chan slid the silencer down over the M14's barrel, and screwed it into place. He slammed a 20-round magazine into it and jacked a round into the chamber.

"When do you think the fun will start?" Chan asked, adjusting his yellow shooter's glasses.

"It may not start at all," Mamudi observed. Outside, there was the sound of angry voices. A moment later, loud shots echoed through the train station.

"Then again. . ." Mamudi snapped as he moved into position. Kinski and Chan slipped into their assigned battle stations and waited for the assault that would surely follow.

• • •

Shostakovic could see the four other assassins moving toward the rail car. He needed to keep the crowd's attention focused on him. He fired the pistol into the air and screamed. The train station was in an uproar. Everyone dropped to the floor to avoid any stray rounds. Nearby, the man and his wife cowered behind an iron column. Shostakovic ran up to them, screaming.

"Don't have a fiver for me, eh?" he shrieked. "Well have this then!" He raised the pistol and aimed between the woman's eyes.

She screamed and closed her eyes, jerking her hands up over her face. Shostakovic smiled. There was nothing so gratifying as seeing fear on a woman's face, except maybe watching her die. Her husband cowered next to her, pleading uselessly for their miserable lives. He would be next.

Shostakovic's enjoyment was curtailed by a 7.62mm boattail that slowed down only briefly as it blew his head apart like a melon left in a campfire. His nearly headless body stood there for a moment as the contents of his skull, now a wet pink mist, drifted slowly toward the open doors of Victoria Station.

"Nice shot, Buddha," Kinski snapped. "Here come his buddies!"

Outside, four men ran toward the car. They were dressed in railroad worker's uniforms, but the Czech Skorpion machine pistols gave away their real occupation.

The four men split into two pairs and jumped onto the platform at each end of the car. In a perfectly choreographed move, one man at each end smashed the glass with his weapon as the other threw in a concussion grenade. The grenades went off with a roar and a shower of hot sparks. Before the sound could echo, the killers were in the car, shooting in every direction. It took them a second to realize that the car was empty. Then a voice spoke from above.

"Hello, suckers!"

The killers looked up to see three men braced against the ceiling. The tiny MP5K's stuttered to life, their 9mm slugs ripping into the assassin team. Their roaring covered the cough of Chan's rifle as it gouged chunks of flesh from the spinning, twitching slimebags below. In two seconds, the four men were dead. Indeed, they were beyond dead; they were disintegrated.

Chan was the first to slip down from his perch.

He bent down to the most intact assassin, then looked back up.

"Keenan's going to be pissed!" he said as he took off the yellow glasses and placed them carefully in his breast pocket.

"Why?" Kinski asked, as he dropped down beside Chan.

"We were supposed to take a prisoner!" Mamudi reminded his friend as he, too, dropped back to the bloodstained carpet.

"Oh, yeah," Kinski whined, "I forgot!" He looked at the other two Marauders. The three were silent for a moment, then Kinski snapped his fingers in mock irritation.

"I hate it when I do that!" he said. All three burst out laughing.

The crowd of terrified passengers swirled past him as they fled the gunfire in the station. Butakov stood next to a pay phone, the handle held near his ear. The buzz of the dial tone went unnoticed in the din. He saw Shostakovic die, then watched as the team assaulted the king's car. There was a flurry of shooting in the car followed by a moment of silence then another round of firing, louder this time.

A few moments later, three men emerged from the rail car. They were not his men. Butakov turned and joined the throng of fleeing passengers. He had seen enough. They had been fooled here. The king's guards were alerted. They would have to take him at Balmoral now.

FIVE

The first two divers were down for thirty minutes securing the lifting rig to the the weapons loading hatch. When they emerged, the other two divers went down to continue the task. To prevent the bends, neither team stayed down too long.

By mid-afternoon, the hoisting line was secure and ready to haul up the missiles. Müeller called a halt at that point and the crew quit for the day so the divers could decompress overnight. They would be down longer the next day, bringing up the first missile.

Kruger was impatient. As they motored back to the hotel dock, he stood on the bow, drumming his fingers on the gunwale. The work was progressing right on schedule, but Kruger wanted it finished. He looked over his shoulders at the others. They were all jovial, even the divers who sat wrapped in blankets sipping brandy brought along from the hotel bar. Müeller seemed ecstatic.

Dreaming of gold, Kruger suspected. Well, he thought, dream on, moron. He looked ahead again, searching for the inlet.

I'm so keyed-up, he mused, I'd like to get drunk, but I can't. I need to be sharp tomorrow when those bozos bring up that nuke. A seagull landed on the gunwale a few feet away. Kruger turned toward it.

"I hate delayed gratification!" he explained to the large sea bird, which squawked earnestly in agreement.

The sun was still high when the inlet and the hotel hove into view. As the crew tied up the launch, Kruger jumped onto the dock and made for the hotel.

As he stomped through the front door into the tiny lobby, Kruger saw a flash of dark hair disappear through the door that led to the hotel kitchen. He smiled. The hotel keeper's wife was still around during the day. That idea warmed him. He would have to get to know her better before they left with the missiles.

Thinking about her made his loins stir and he went into the public bar for some whiskey to feed the feeling, ignoring his earlier concern for sobriety.

Several grizzled locals were drowning themselves in the hotel's watered down beer. In the only booth, a red-faced merchant was sweet-talking a buxom tart with no apparent success. The other bar patrons sat chuckling in their beer at him. The hotel owner was tending bar.

As Kruger approached the bar, the conversation fell off.

"Whiskey," Kruger ordered, "real whiskey, not that local poison!"

The owner opened a cabinet below the bar, pulled out a bottle of Johnny Walker Red and set it on the bar with a shot glass. Kruger knocked away the shot glass and took a swig from the bottle, watching the other patrons' reaction. Most seemed jealous. Few could afford the costly spirits that had been plentiful before the war. The tart in the back booth was the only one who didn't seem resentful. She smiled and slid out of the booth, pushing the merchant away. Her hips swayed provocatively as she slowly crossed the room and leaned against the bar. She leaned forward to give Kruger a better view of her pillow-like breasts, which were barely contained by the loose, elastic top of her dress.

"How about a bit of that for a thirsty girl?" she cooed.

Kruger smiled and reached for the discarded shot glass. He poured it full of the tawny liquid and slid the glass toward her. She picked it up and held it to her full lower lip. She looked up at Kruger, smiled and tossed back the scotch. She made a face and shook all over as the liquor warmed her insides.

"I'm Natalie," she purred. "That was tasty."

"There's more," Kruger answered, taking another swig from the bottle. He turned to the owner. "Put this on my tab," he sneered. Kruger smiled at the girl and started toward the door. He stopped there and looked back at her. She glanced quickly at her former companion, gave him a mean little smile, and followed Kruger out the door.

In his room, Natalie was a coquettish tease, trading peeks and squeezes for sips from his bottle. It amused Kruger to play this game because he already knew how it would end.

By the time the bottle was empty, she was flushed and had a wild eager look on her face. Kruger pulled her to him and roughly jerked the top of her dress. Her abundant breasts toppled free and she tried to cover them with her arms.

"No," Kruger snapped as he grabbed her wrists and twisted them to her sides. He smiled wolfishly at her as he spun her around and tossed her roughly onto the bed. She sat up on her elbows as he pulled the web belt loose from his pants, her eyes wide with fear and excitement.

"You bad girl, you've drunk all my whiskey," he hissed. "I think you need to be punished!" He wrapped the belt once around his hand, then snapped it taut.

"No!" she cried, scrunching herself up against the wall, "please . . ."

"That's right," Kruger said as he stepped up to the bed, "beg!"

"Oh, please!" Natalie squealed. Kruger was only slightly disconcerted by the wicked little smile that suddenly played around the corners of her wide, red mouth.

Oh, well, he thought. He laughed as he drew back the belt.

The next morning dawned clear and calm, perfect for recovering the missiles. Müeller and the others were surprised to see Kruger whistling and smiling as he stepped off the dock onto the Ariel.

"You're quite chipper this morning," Müeller observed.

"Indeed," Kruger agreed. "Nothing like a couple of stiff belts to pick up your spirits!" He laughed at his own pun, causing great confusion among the others who had never seen the man so jovial. His cheerful attitude continued unabated as they motored out to the recovery site.

The first missile came up just after noon. Kruger held his breath as the long cylinder broke the surface and the crew winched it aboard and lowered it gently into its waiting rack.

An accident at this point would be a disaster. The chairman was unlikely to forgive any mistake on this project. If he lost even one of the missiles,. Kruger knew he would envy the dead men on the Soviet sub they were looting.

His fears were groundless. The first missile was soon securely nestled in its rack. There were no apparent leaks or cracks in the cannister. So far, so good.

"Well," the watcher asked his companion, "is it time to transmit?"

The other man nodded. The two men slid back down the rise, started the small motorcycle and rode away.

An hour later, they stepped into a clearing several kilometers from the coast and set up a small antenna that looked like it was made of old venetian blind parts. The four wide blades were held together by a thin wire circle. It sat on a small tripod, the blades facing up like a skeletal metal flower seeking the sun.

One of the men took out a compass and watched the dial for a moment. He reached down and turned the tiny antenna a few degrees to the right, then nodded to his partner who knelt next to a dark green box that seemed a cross between a small computer and a military radio. At his friend's nodded signal, he silently pressed a key on the small computer keyboard. The two men waited for ten minutes, then closed up the odd radio and folded the small antenna.

"We will try again after dark," the taller man said as he slipped the antenna into a canvas bag. His friend nodded agreement as they disappeared back into the woods.

SIX

Balmoral Castle sat atop a bleak Scottish hill like a square lighthouse in a sea of heather. From its ramparts, you could see for miles around. The wind whipped around Keenan and the three others as they surveyed the unadorned landscape. The others pulled their jackets closer around them, but Keenan was oblivious to the cold. The wind seemed to energize him, making his skin tingle.

"Is this a godforsaken spot or what?" Kinski muttered, "I almost hope they do attack soon so we don't freeze our butts off up here."

Buddha Chan was scanning the horizon with a small pocket monocular and smiling broadly. "Except for the wind," he said, "this place is a sniper's paradise!" He turned to the others, his eyes squinted up into two slits by the big grin that slashed across his face.

"They'll have to be ghosts to get in here!" Kinski trilled, "this ought to be easy duty!"

"I wonder," Mamudi said quietly. "True, it will be hard to get to the king, but we are trapped here, too."

Keenan looked around at the Afghan and smiled. "But the best defense is a good offense, eh, Freddie?"

"Exactly!" Mamudi smiled.

Shatterhand was furious. "I am not going out in this get-up!" he roared, shaking the heavy bullet-proof vest at Callahan and the three Marauders who stood nearby, amused by the show.

"Whose idea was this anyhow?" Shatterhand snarled. "I

31

didn't want to come up here in the first place, now I have to go out like a medieval knight in an armor suit!"

"It was mine, Your Grace," Callahan replied. "You're supposed to be up here to do some grouse shooting. After you go out today, we'll announce that you have a cold and are staying up here until you feel better."

Shatterhand rolled his eyes and rubbed his forehead with the back of the black glove that covered his twisted hand.

"The point is to make these thugs come in to get you," Mamudi explained, "so we can deal with them."

"So that makes me the bait, eh?" Shatterhand snapped. Mamudi held up his palms and shrugged.

"Where's that red-headed maniac of yours, anyway?" Shatterhand asked as he struggled into the armor.

"Hunting," Chan answered, "slime hunting."

On the long drive to Scotland, Butakov went over the plan again and again.

One team would cause a diversion while the other team assaulted Shatterhand's quarters in the dead of night. Spartacus had provided them with floor plans of the castle, identity papers that would pass casual inspection and two vehicles, a Land Rover and a lumpy English van. Another FSE spy would help them once they got to Scotland.

The knowledge that this plan was alarmingly similar to the plan that had just failed troubled him, but there was little time to devise another one. Besides, his troops were not gifted thinkers. Any change of plan would only confuse and irritate them. As he looked at the castle plans, Butakov secretly prepared an escape route for himself, just in case.

The two teams would be smuggled inside the castle by their spy contact. Two men from one team would start a ruckus in the courtyard outside and draw off the bulk of the guards. The others would assault Shatterhand's quarters, kill the guards and then the king. Simple.

Crazy Jack Keenan sat looking out the window of the pub at the dark clouds. A fine drizzle of water peppered the glass, turning the view down the tiny village's broad street into a psychedelic vision. From time to time, Keenan let the toxin's effect on his vision go unchecked. The result was a phantasmagoria of colors and textures unseen by normal eyes. He could see into both the infrared and ultraviolet spectrums, but the ultraviolet produced pain, and he avoided it, if possible.

He sat grooving on his in-house trip as the van turned up the street and passed the pub. As it passed, a feeling of dread mixed with excitement came over him. Something in that van had yanked his sixth sense. By the time he lurched up out of his chair and got to the door, the van was gone, lost in the labyrinth of tiny winding streets.

Jack stood in the door, rain streaking down his face and soaking his light jacket. Whoever they were, they were here. It would begin soon.

The address on Limerick Street was a rusty metal building set back off the street. As they drove into the short driveway, the metal roll-up door opened. Butakov drove in, parking his Rover at the far end of the large dark room. Behind them, a figure silhouetted against the thin light from outside pulled the door back down.

Butakov walked back toward the entrance as the door came down and the FSE agent turned toward him. For a second, Butakov's eyes seemed to be playing tricks on him. The agent was a woman, one of the most beautiful he had ever seen.

"Maggie Steele," she said, extending her hand. Butakov shook it. Her grip was firm.

"Butakov," he answered.

"Where are the others?" she asked, looking past him at the four men who were loitering around the Rover.

"They'll be along," he answered.

"Right," she went on, "well until they are, you can make yourself at home." She pointed at the loft overhead. "There's bunks up there and a sink to wash in." She started for the door. "I'll be back after dark to brief you. Stay put until then."

Butakov nodded and gestured to the men to put their things away upstairs. He walked over to the grimy window and watched her walk back toward the town centre.

Hardly what I expected as an agent, he thought, but then, that's what made a good agent, after all.

"They're here," Keenan said brightly. "A van full of 'em!"

"How do you know, Jack?" Callahan asked, rising from the overstuffed wing chair.

"Trust me," Crazy Jack answered. "It's them!"

"Jack can smell 'em a mile off!" Buddha Chan laughed.

"Hear 'em two miles off," Kinski promised.

Mamudi crossed the room and stood next to the red haired giant. "Jack has the ability, the power, if you will, to sense things," Mamudi explained. "He can feel the presence of danger."

"The force," Kinski added somberly, "is with him."

Callahan ignored the two jokers and studied Keenan. "How many?" he asked. "Could you tell?"

"Several," Keenan answered. "Don't know how many for sure, but more than a couple."

"At least that's a start," Callahan replied, "I'll order a troop of soldiers up here immediately. We'll button up the place."

"No," Keenan snapped, shaking his head, "if you do that, they'll just hole up somewhere and wait. Sooner or later, the king will be vulnerable and then they'll strike."

"What do you propose?" Callahan asked, skeptically.

"Invite 'em in," Keenan replied.

As a look of extreme skepticism swept over Callahan, Mamudi jumped into the conversation. "Of course," he interrupted, "it is easier to lead the jackal into the trap than to track him in the brush." Callahan shot the zipper-faced man a look of confusion, then went back to his conversation with Keenan.

"How do you propose to keep the king safe?" he asked.

"Does this place have a dungeon?" Keenan asked.

"Of course," Callahan replied, "all castles this size have a dungeon."

"Then lock him up!" Keenan explained.

"What? Lock up the king?" Callahan asked, "are you out of your mind?"

"Definitely!" Keenan answered.

When she got back to the pub, Maggie Steele quickly scanned the interior of the bar. The big red-haired stranger was gone.

Too bad, she thought, he was really something. He had an aura around him that she found very attractive. Besides, anyone that tall and that big had to have something serious in his trousers!

She knew he was one of the king's men. Still, that didn't make him unattractive. He was friendly enough, too. It would be a shame if he got killed. An idea suddenly flashed in her

mind. Perhaps the big stranger could be the ticket to the castle!
She smiled at the prospect of confirming her suspicion about
the big man's equipment.

"What does it mean?" Shatterhand asked Signals Master
Donovan as he read the short message again.

"I think it is self-explanatory," the head of the royal radio
section answered. "What I wonder is who sent it, and why."

The message itself was simple: FSE recovering Soviet SS-
NX-21 cruise missiles in Baltic Sea.

A set of map coordinates followed the text. The message was
repeated several times. It had been transmitted twice, several
hours apart.

Shatterhand looked out the tall, leaded windows. Outside,
shafts of sunlight knifed through the thick clouds, brilliantly
lighting the green fields around the castle against the dark sky.
Like those fields, England was a land brightly lit by freedom's
light and surrounded by the dark clouds of oppression. He felt
a chill inside as he realized that like the fields which faded
from light to dark, so could the light of freedom be quickly
extinguished here, too.

The Soviet missiles could finish the job the war had started.
Nuclear blasts on their island nation, so weakened by the big
Nuke-Out, would destroy their will to fight. No one could fight
nukes. That had been amply demonstrated.

Maximov's thugs could prevail without even firing the
missiles. Just the threat of nuclear bombs could be enough
to enable the FSE to take over. There was no counter force
to retaliate with. Or was there?

Maximov's plans had been thwarted before by the toughest,
most unpredictable force in Europe—the Marauders. If ever
there had been a job for those wild men, this was it. Shatterhand
folded the message and walked across the room.

He opened the heavy wood door. Buddha Chan, leaning on
the door outside, nearly fell onto the king.

"Sorry your Kingship," Chan stammered, regaining his balance. Shatterhand sighed. As bodyguards, the Marauders were
getting to be like a tight shirt. He could hardly turn around
without running into one of them. It wouldn't be so bad if they
weren't so obnoxious and disrespectful!

"Where's your boss?" Shatterhand asked the Mongol.

"In town, nosing around," Buddha answered.

"Get him!" Shatterhand barked.

"Sir," Chan came to attention and rendered a snappy salute. "Yes, sir!" The blocky sniper did a quick about face and disappeared. Outside the door, Kinski peered around, his AKM cradled in his arms.

"Something up?" he asked casually.

"Perhaps," Shatterhand answered as he firmly shut the door. He returned to the small table where Donovan waited.

"Who do you think sent this message?" Shatterhand asked his signals expert.

"Someone who knows how to set up a satellite antenna and knows where the satellite is in the sky," Donovan speculated. "Only NATO special operations troops used radios on that frequency."

"Do you think any of them could have survived?" Shatterhand asked.

"Perhaps," Donovan replied, "or some partisans that were trained by them."

Shatterhand sat, silently studying the black glove that covered his ruined hand. The message could be bait to lure the Marauders away from him, so that the assassins could succeed. On the other hand, he thought, looking at his good hand, the assassins may be here to keep them nailed down. Either way, the risk was great, but nuclear blackmail was worse than simple assassination. The Marauders would have to find the message's sender, and then destroy the missiles before Maximov could use them. If something happened to him—well, there were others to take his place.

Maggie set the warm beer in front of the red-haired giant and sat in the chair opposite him across the small round table. He smiled at her as he drank half the pint in one deep gulp.

"So you're with the king's people up at the castle?" she asked, never taking her eyes from his. The big man nodded in mid-gulp.

"Coldstream, are you?" she asked, referring to the elite Coldstream Guards that had guarded the British royal family for generations.

"Hardly," he answered, wiping his mouth with the back of his hand.

"You sound like a Yank," she observed. She saw the slightest flicker behind his eyes.

"That's right," he said, setting the empty glass down on the little table.

"My Dad served with some Yanks before the war," Maggie went on. "I've got some pictures of him and his Yank buddies. Would you like to see them?"

He looked at her for a long second. There was something about her that set off his danger alarms, but he could not tell if she was a physical danger or more an emotional threat. Only one way to find out.

"Yeah," he answered, "I'd like that." She stood and led him through the pub to the narrow spiral staircase that led to the living quarters above.

Her room was larger than he expected, actually two rooms connected by a bathroom. They were barely in the door when she spun and wrapped her arms around his neck and drew him down into a deep soul kiss that sent electric jolts throughout his body, especially one central area. When they finally broke for air, he leaned back and asked, "What about those photos?"

"I lied," she whispered, "I just wanted you up here. My dad never even met any Yanks, I think." She glued her lips to his again to stifle any more conversation.

Keenan let his hands explore her back, her sensuous hips and her taut buns. She groaned and gasped in response, grinding her sex against his.

Finally, she broke the clinch and took his hand, guiding him to her quilt-covered bed. She sat on the edge of the bed and began to unlace the top of her dress. Keenan could see her large nipples protruding through the fabric. She was talking to him, her voice low and sexy.

Keenan would have liked to hear what she was saying but the warning alarms in his head were ringing so loudly, he couldn't hear himself think.

So just don't think, he advised himself, go with the flow and see where it carries you.

"Seen a big, red-headed American in here?" Chan asked the bartender in the dark pub. The man jerked his thumb toward the corner of the room where a spiral staircase led up. Chan bolted up the stairs and stood looking at the two doors at the top of the stairs.

From behind the door on the right, Crazy Jack Keenan's voice cried out, a strangled, tortured sound. Chan twisted the knob and slammed his considerable bulk against the door. It was unlocked. Chan sprawled into the room, rolling to his feet in a crouch at the foot of the bed.

In the bed, Jack Keenan was still crying out, though obviously not as a result of any torture. Keenan was twisting around, wide-eyed with surprise. Beneath him, the cries of an equally wide-eyed woman turned from pleasure to terror, as a bald bullet of a man appeared at the foot of her bed. She began to clutch frantically at the bed sheets.

Keenan twisted around to face the intruder, his face contorted with surprise and irritation.

"Buddha!" he screamed, "what the fuck are you doing?"

"I, I mean, the king wants you," the embarrassed Mongol stammered.

Keenan sat up in the bed as his companion pulled the sheets up around her neck.

"Anybody ever talk to you about your timing?" he shouted. Chan sat down against the wall, trying to hide his embarrassment.

"Sorry about that, Jack," he said, a smile spreading across his wide face, "I thought you were in trouble!"

"Well, he bloody well wasn't, was he?" the woman shrieked, "not until you crashed the party!" She glared at the squat man squatting at the foot of her bed. If looks could have killed, Buddha Chan would have been sushi.

Keenan rubbed his face and rolled off the bed, reaching for his pants. He dressed in silence as Maggie continued to glare at Chan, who now stood nervously facing the still open door.

Keenan pulled his boots on and sat back down on the bed.

"Sorry," he said, stroking her face. He looked over at Chan. "I guess introductions are in order. Maggie Steele, this is Winston S. Chan." Chan waved back over his shoulder, still staring out the door. Maggie pulled one hand out from under the sheet and made an obscene gesture. "Charmed, I'm sure!" she said, her words dripping vitriol.

Keenan kissed her cheek and stood. "I'll be back."

"Yeah, sure," she said, rolling her eyes toward the wall.

Keenan and Chan made as graceful an exit as possible under the circumstances.

"Thank you so much," Keenan growled sarcastically as they clumped down the spiral staircase, "what's so damned important?" He suddenly grew serious. "Is the king . . ."

"He's okay," Chan said. "Later, outside." The two men walked to Chan's waiting Morris Mini. Keenan forced his huge bulk into the tiny car.

"This thing sucks!" Keenan complained, his knees firmly locked under his chin.

"I dunno," Chan disagreed, "it fits me just fine!"

"Runt!" Keenan grumbled. They rode for a moment in silence. Finally, Chan couldn't keep back the question.

"So how was it?" he asked.

"Aside from the abrupt finish," Keenan snarled, "it was unbelievable!" A smile spread across his big face. "You bastard! I get my first cosmic piece of ass and here you come, Sergeant Birth Control!"

Chan laughed and Keenan joined him. They laughed all the way back to the castle.

"So how was the big man?" Butakov sneered as Maggie combed her hair back into shape.

"That's none of your bleedin' concern is it?" she replied. "Are your men ready?"

"Always," he answered, eyeing her lush figure from where he sat on her still warm bed, "just like their leader."

She saw his leer in the mirror and turned around to face him. "Forget it," she advised. As he shrugged, she stepped over to the small closet and took out the black coveralls. She slipped the jumpsuit on under her robe, then turned her back to Butakov and dropped her robe to the floor. He studied her bare back and the flash of breast on one side as she pulled the coveralls up and zipped them.

"You're here to do a job," she reminded him, "if you complete it, then maybe we'll talk."

Butakov just laughed and got up from the bed as she pulled a nylon day pack out from under her bed and shouldered it. "Let's go," she said, leading the way out the door.

SEVEN

"Missiles!" Keenan exclaimed. "I thought both sides used them all during the Nuke-Out!"

"It was our belief that those missiles not actually fired during the conflict were either destroyed by enemy action or unrecoverable," Ian McMillan, the retired English general who served as Shatterhand's military expert on the old Soviet military machine, explained. "Most of the unrecoverable ones are in sunken submarines from both sides."

"These appear to have been recovered from a sunken Soviet sub," Shatterhand added. He looked out the window at the dark clouds. "If they are real, they are the only known operational nuclear weapons." He looked at the four Americans. "If Maximov controls them," he added, "he will be able to blackmail the world with them."

"With a couple of crummy cruise missiles?" Kinski interrupted.

"Yes," Shatterhand said. "No one would be willing to be the first target. Besides, we don't know if there are one, two, or a full load of missiles on the sub." He turned to McMillan.

"A Soviet attack sub could carry as many as a dozen SS-NX-21 missiles," the thin, white-haired gentleman, explained. "That would be a considerable nuclear arsenal today."

"As they say in the movies, let's cut to the chase," Mamudi interrupted. "You want us to go after the missiles, am I correct?"

Before Shatterhand could answer, Keenan spoke.

"No way!" He pointed over his shoulder toward the village. "There are folks right down there in town waiting to kill your highness! We're not going anywhere!"

Shatterhand walked over and sat on the edge of the large, carved desk. "That is the problem, isn't it?" he replied. "It's possible that this message is a ruse to draw you off so those thugs can get to me. On the other hand, this assassination business could be the ruse meant to tie you down so you cannot interfere with the recovery of the missiles."

"So why don't we just split up?" Kinski asked. "Me and Freddie here can deal with these slimeballs. Jack and Buddha could go take those missiles out!"

"No," Mamudi answered. "We should not split up the team. Our strength comes from unity."

"Oh, bullshit," Kinski argued. "Our strength comes from being damn good at what we do, not from some cosmic crap."

Keenan suddenly walked over to the window and pressed his forehead to the glass. He stood that way with his eyes closed for a moment, then turned and flashed a wolfish grin. "Maybe we won't have to split the team," he said quietly, "I gotta feeling we'll be through here very soon."

BRRAAAP!

"I'll kill you myself if you fart again!" Butakov hissed. The five men and their weapons were jammed into the tiny space under the false floor of the van, and they were gagging on the trapped noxious odor.

Harley's evil chuckle revealed him as the culprit.

Later, my English friend, Butakov mused, smiling to himself. He planned to kill Harley and Flanagan after the mission and leave them for the English authorities to find. The IRA would get the blame for the king's murder, sowing discord between the English and Irish again. Two birds with one stone, as the English would say.

"Quiet!" Maggie called from the driver's seat. "We're nearly there!"

The van slowed as it neared the castle gate. The guards would not be suspicious, the van came every evening with the fresh food and supplies for the castle.

Maggie frequently drove the van. The guards were always glad to see her. She flirted shamelessly with them and frequently wore clothes that showed off her breasts. The zipper on her coveralls was down halfway to her navel for just that purpose. Hopefully, the one on duty would just wave her through. If the guard at the gate acted up on her, though, she had a silenced pistol tucked under her leg to deal with him.

As she neared the gate, she saw young Smythe on duty. Smythe liked her and his face lit up when he recognized her. As she stopped, he stepped over to the van window.

"So, Maggie," he said brightly, "how goes it, darling?"

She turned in the seat, exposing most of her large left breast to his view. "Boring, as usual," she sighed. "I need a real man to perk up my dreary life!"

"You know where I am!" he eagerly volunteered.

"I do indeed," she teased. "By yourself, tonight?"

"Yeah, 'till midnight," he answered. "Come back and keep me company."

"Maybe I will," she said as he stepped back for her to pass. She gunned the van toward the large kitchen door on one side of the castle keep.

"They're here," Jack Keenan said a second before the phone burred to announce that the van had entered the castle. The other three Marauders each picked up his weapon and slammed a round into its chamber.

"Let's do it!" Chan bubbled, fitting his yellow shooters glasses over the slits that were his eyes. A feral smile split his face.

The assassins would most likely enter through the kitchen, expecting to find only a cook waiting to unload the food and supplies, but there would be a surprise for them tonight.

Chan stayed on the stairway that faced the castle gate. From the window, he could see the gate and the road beyond. The diversion, if there was one, would surely come from the gate. Chan could handle it.

Keenan, Mamudi and Kinski would handle the slimers in the van.

As she pulled up to the big double door, Maggie zipped the coveralls up and pulled a black watch cap on over her head.

When the cook opened the sliding door behind her, Maggie would pop her on the head with her gun butt and push her into the van. That would clear the way into the big storeroom that led to the kitchen. The cook could be used as a human shield if they needed one to escape.

In the back of the van, the five killers emerged from their tiny hiding place, quickly stretching their cramped muscles to restore circulation. They crouched behind the crates in the back of the van, waiting for Maggie to cue them to launch the attack.

Once inside the storeroom, the assassin team would make its way toward the office suite where Shatterhand worked until midnight each night. When the second team attacked the main gate, they would burst into the offices and kill Shatterhand and everyone else there.

Maggie pulled up close to the heavy doors. The doors opened to the inside and she could park the van close enough to keep any prying eyes from seeing her knock out the cook, or from seeing the five men slip from the van into the storeroom.

She stopped the van, but left it running. Easing herself into the back, she slid open the van's side door. The tension in the back of the van was enough to wilt the produce in the crates. She nodded to the others, then knocked on the big door.

There was no answer. That was odd, but not impossible. She turned the large blade-type handle. The door opened. She swung it open and stepped inside. There was no one in the dark storeroom. She crossed it to the kitchen door. It was unlocked. She opened it and looked cautiously into the big kitchen. There was no one there, but a tiny transistor radio was playing on a counter.

Cook must be away for a moment, she thought, so much the better. She turned and gestured to the men in the van. In two seconds, they were out of the van and into the storeroom.

"This will be easy!" Harley hissed in Butakov's ear.

He could hear the men in the kitchen, sense them. There were five of them; violence radiating from them like heat from a radiator. He could feel his own violent will rising within him. It felt like the rush of some powerful amphetamine—urgent, undeniable. He also knew that when it was over, he would feel a deeper peace than at any other time. Either the thrill of victory, or the peace of death. The death part was not too likely. As the rush hit its zenith, Keenan nodded at Kinski.

Kinski pivoted to cover the kitchen door as Keenan sprinted across the huge dining hall. The short run seemed a blur to Keenan. He pressed his back to the cold stone wall, listening beyond the wide door that led to the kitchen. This dining room had hosted kings, prime ministers, tribal chiefs and presidents. Tonight it contained a pack of human rats and three exterminators. The stone wall felt cold, even through his black BDUs. From the corner of his eye, he saw Mamudi start across the hall. In seconds, the wiry Afghan slid to a halt against the far side of the door.

Keenan looked back at Kinski and nodded again. Kinski ran across the hall toward the center of the door. When he was ten feet away, Keenan pivoted and kicked in the kitchen door. As it swung in, Kinski barrelled through it into the kitchen.

Keenan was right behind him, his eyes probing the gloomy room. Their arrival was so sudden, the three men entering the kitchen from the storeroom were caught by surprise. Kinski opened fire on them, moving and firing his MP5K. The three men fired back, their shots going wild as the stream of 9mm lead ripped through their chests, spraying the wall behind them with sanguine pointillism.

Beyond the three, there were more in the storeroom. As Keenan charged the open storeroom door, screaming his hate at the vermin scurrying around in the dark room, he felt another presence, one he knew all too well.

Flame belched from a weapon. Keenan could almost see the slugs as they streaked by inches from his chest. He whirled, walking a long burst across the dark spot where the flame had just been. The diminutive MP5K roared in the stone room, but Keenan could not hear it. The weapon was merely an extension of his own senses. His eyes were like laser sights. Wherever he looked, the 9mm slugs followed.

Two cases of canned tomatoes exploded like vegetable grenades, showering the area with a sticky red spray that mimicked the blood that gushed up from the big man's chest as he slammed backward toward the wall and fell bleeding to the concrete floor.

Keenan didn't notice the mixed media show, he was twisting to avoid a burst that ripped from the side of a stack of canned goods boxes. Keenan fired the rest of his 32 round magazine at the edge of the stack as he picked up speed and slammed into the stacked boxes.

The impact tipped over the stack, toppling the boxes on the man hiding behind.

A heavy case of canned liquid knocked the man down and Keenan was on him like a mongoose on a trapped snake. The man twisted, trying to bring his weapon to bear on Keenan. Crazy Jack executed a fast heel stomp to the side of the man's head and dropped to one knee, seizing the man's weapon and wrenching it from his hand. The man was hissing something about Keenan's mother as Jack twisted the machine pistol from his grip.

Behind him, Mamudi's weapon stuttered, the shots echoing in the room. Someone screamed in the darkness behind him. Keenan knew that Maggie was hit; he hoped she was not dead, even though she had led these slime bags to the king.

The man beneath him was struggling to free himself from the crush of cardboard boxes. Three streams of olive oil from a perforated case were furnishing lubrication. The man grabbed Keenan's leg, nearly pulling him off balance. Keenan bent down to keep his balance, pressed the machine pistol into the hollow at the base of the man's throat and fired. The man's body spasmed as the slugs severed his spine and ricocheted up from the concrete floor to enter his head like a swarm of killer bees. A second later, the man lay still.

The room was suddenly silent except for the painful moans coming from the corner. On the staircase, Buddha Chan's rifle was engaging in a deadly dialog with other weapons outside.

"Kinski," Keenan barked, "give Buddha a hand!" Kinski, checking the bodies in the kitchen for any lingering signs of life, stood, snapped a fresh magazine in his weapon. "Right!" he snapped as he ran back to Buddha's perch on the stairs.

Keenan walked slowly over to the dark figure lying back on a stack of eggs against the corner. The eggs were pulverized, their scrambled contents making the floor around Maggie a slippery slew.

Keenan knelt next to her and put his hand under her head. She opened her eyes and smiled at him.

"Hello, Jack," she whispered. "Sorry."

"Why, Maggie?" Keenan asked. "Why you?"

"Old IRA family, Jack," she whispered, her voice becoming weaker. "It's in the blood, you know." She tried to laugh, but began coughing instead, a trickle of blood running down her pale cheek into her hair.

Behind him, Mamudi put a hand on Keenan's shoulder.

"Jack . . ." he said softly.

Keenan waved his hand to say "later." Mamudi stepped back.

Maggie's coughing subsided and she looked up at Keenan again, weakly trying to smile.

"I'm dying, Jack," she whispered.

"I know, babe," he answered.

"Would you hold me?" she pleaded. Keenan sat next to her in the wet mass of broken eggs. She moaned as he pulled her up and put his arm under her, pulling her close to him. She reached up to touch his face but didn't have the strength. He took her hand and held it to his face. She smiled again, then her eyes seemed to look past him into a world only the dead can see. She went limp in his arms, her breath rushing out into his face. He felt the life leave her, held her body for a moment longer then lowered her back down.

"Jack . . ." Mamudi began again, his voice apologetic.

"She was one of them, Freddie," Keenan answered. "Save the sympathy." Keenan walked back over to the dead man who still lay under the case of cans.

"Here is the leader," Keenan said. "I could feel it."

"You are quite a salad chef, Jack," Mamudi observed, switching on the light. Keenan's first victim lay in a welter of romaine lettuce from a case he had collapsed upon. All over him and the crushed lettuce was a thick mixture of splattered tomatoes and hemoglobin dressing.

"This reminds me of dish from my homeland," Mamudi said, fingering his zipper-like scar.

"Oh, please," Keenan said, taking the twisted gourmet by the arm and pulling him along to see how Chan and Kinski were doing on the stairs.

The steady booming of Chan's M14 greeted them as they entered the dining hall. The rattle of Kinski's MP5K filled the gaps between the sniper rifle booms. As Keenan and

Mamudi mounted the stairs, the firing above stopped. The sudden silence was almost as deafening as the shooting.

"Buddha, Kinski," Keenan called, "how you doin'?"

Kinski's lanky form appeared on the steps above them. "It's all over here, boss," he reported, running the metal comb through his badly damaged pompadour. "Buddha hogged them all!"

"You just couldn't hit any of them with that pipsqueak peashooter," Chan disagreed, "but thanks for keeping them occupied."

Kinski sneered, Mamudi laughed, and Keenan felt another rush sweep over him. This feeling, unbidden, uncontrollable, was one of mixed triumph and disappointment. They had saved the king, but now it was over and Keenan was sorry. The thought of Maggie's body lying in the eggshells brought another pang. Keenan sat down on the stairs and leaned against the wall.

"Hey, bossman," Kinski called from the foot of the stairs, "wanta come have a look at the others?"

"You two go on out," Mamudi answered. "We'll follow." He sat next to his suddenly quiet friend.

"God save the king, Jack," Mamudi said quietly. "Sorry about the woman."

Keenan shook his head. "God save us all, Freddie," he answered. The castle staff was beginning to emerge from their hiding places in the bowels of castle. Outside, a police car's singsong siren signaled its progress from the village.

"Come on, Jack," Mamudi urged the shaking red-haired giant, "let's see to Shatterhand."

Keenan nodded and stood up. The two men walked slowly down the stairs and were engulfed by the grateful castle staff.

A few moments later, Shatterhand, McMillan and Donovan emerged from the bowels of the castle dungeon.

"It's all over, Your Highness," Kinski blurted.

"We smoked 'em!" Chan agreed, still high from his long distance ambush of the diversionary party.

Shatterhand walked up to Keenan, who was distractedly staring out the tall windows.

"Let me see them," he said. Keenan looked around at the former cop turned king.

"They're not pretty," Keenan answered. He turned and walked toward the blasted storeroom. The king and his party followed.

The storeroom was thick with the sweet smell of death. Shatterhand looked at each corpse, stopping to look longer at Butakov.

"This one looks familiar," he observed.

McMillan stared at the assassin's now peaceful face.

"Butakov," he identified the dead man, "One of Maximov's best, or worst, depending how you look at it."

"There were five more outside," Kinski interrupted, "Buddha and I got them!" Chan shot Kinski a look, but let it go.

"One thing," Keenan added, "they had inside help up here." He pointed at Maggie's still body. "They had to have help in London, too."

Shatterhand looked quickly at McMillan, who nodded. "We'll find our traitor, Jack." He turned and left the kitchen, walking silently up to his office with the four Americans in tow. When they were behind the massive oak doors, Shatterhand spoke again.

"I am convinced that all this was just to keep you four pinned down here," he began. "Maximov has nukes and wants to get them into action without your interference." The king took a cigarette from a small carved box on the table and lit it. Keenan noticed the tremor in the king's good hand. When the smoke was lit, he looked back up at them.

"I want you four to take out those nukes," he said flatly. "With them, Maximov can bully the world into submission."

"Any idea where they are?" Keenan asked.

"Northern Germany, near the Baltic Sea," Donovan, the radio chief, answered. "We have coordinates."

"Then let's do it!" Kinski snapped. The others nodded their agreement.

Be very careful what you wish for, Keenan thought, for you will surely get it!

EIGHT

When the second missile came out of the water, Kruger could not contain his relief.

"Yes!" he exclaimed. "Yes!" He almost danced a little jig on the Ariel's deck as the second SS-NX-21 gently settled into the deck rack.

Kruger walked over as Müeller's deck crew strapped the missile cannister in place.

"A great day for the FSE, eh, Kruger," Müeller shouted. He patted the missile like a father patting a favorite son.

Kruger ran his hand over the cold metal tube.

Odd, he thought, how such a cold, wet tube can hold the fire of the sun in it.

"A great day indeed, Müeller," he answered. "You have done well. Very well."

Müeller beamed. The expectation of reward was clear on his weathered face. "I serve the FSE!" he said, parroting the old Soviet military saying.

"And you shall be rewarded," Kruger emphasized. The old man was ecstatic. He sang all the way back to the hotel dock.

The sun was high in the sky when the Ariel tied up at the dock. Kruger left Müeller in charge of the missile and went back to the hotel for some lunch. Afterward, they would load the missiles on a truck and set out for the Schloss Adler.

Stepping through the hotel door, he almost ran head on into

Ulle, the hotel owner's wife. Before she could flee, he caught her wrist.

"Well, hello," he said, holding her wrist in a vice-like grip. "It's nice to see you again. I didn't think we'd see you before we left." He pulled her toward the tiny dining room.

"Why don't you join me for a bite of lunch?" he hissed as she struggled. He twisted her arm up behind her back and forced her forward.

"INNKEEPER!" Kruger bellowed as he and his struggling captive entered the dining room. He forced her into a chair and pushed the table against her, pinning her to the dark paneled wall.

"INNKEEPER!" he bellowed again, "We need some food!"

Keller hustled out of the kitchen, wiping his hands on a apron. He stopped short when he saw Ulle in Kruger's grasp.

"What do you think you are doing?" Keller shouted. He quieted down when he saw the look on her face.

"Your charming wife and I want some lunch!" Kruger ordered. "Something tasty, like her!"

Her eyes pleaded with her husband to go along with the FSE man. Where the FSE was concerned, resistance was always met with violence.

"Yes, Hans," she pleaded. "Get us some of the roast. It's excellent today." The terrified look on her face wrenched his heart. He nodded and turned back to the kitchen.

"Bring some wine, too!" Kruger shouted as Keller disappeared into the kitchen. He turned to his captive. Her hand was turning blue from the iron grip on it. He loosened his hold and she gasped in relief, rubbing her wrist and trying to smile.

Kruger put an arm around her and pulled her to him. "How about a little kiss while we're waiting?"

She struggled for a moment, then allowed him to kiss her. His breath was hot on her face and his lips covered her whole mouth, his tongue forcing its way into her mouth. She fought the urge to gag.

Kruger's hand was exploring the bodice of her dress, kneading the soft flesh beneath. She squirmed in his grasp, but her resistance seemed to make him even more excited. She stifled a scream as he pinched her left nipple hard.

Keller's entrance from the kitchen interrupted his wife's ordeal. When he saw Kruger's hands on her, a flood of emotion

swept over his face. He stifled it and said as calmly as he could,
"Here is your lunch, Herr Kruger."

"Excellent!" Kruger laughed as he released Ulle's tortured
breast. "You're very prompt, my host!"

Keller set down his tray and placed plates in front of Kruger
and his wife. He opened the bottle of wine and poured them
each a glass. Kruger reached for the wine, then paused as
Keller set down the serving tray heaped with roast beef, carrots
and a few small potatoes.

"This roast looks great!" he said. Both Keller and his wife
nodded meekly. Kruger unsnapped his pistol and brought it up
to Ulle's head.

"Perhaps you should join us," he hissed. "Eat!"

Keller looked stricken and his wife cried out. Kruger got an
arm around her neck and pushed the pistol into her ear. "EAT!"
he barked.

A very pathetic look came over Keller. He reached for a
fork and pulled loose a piece of roast. His wife, her mouth
covered by Kruger's hand, whimpered and pleaded with her
eyes. Keller slowly raised the food to his mouth, looking like
a condemned man. He put the roast in his mouth and chewed
it slowly, his eyes shut tight. Ulle struggled in Kruger's grip,
trying to speak to her husband.

Keller chewed the food for a moment, then his eyes grew
wide and he suddenly convulsed, his hands gripping his guts.

Ulle screamed. Kruger cut short her scream with the butt of
his pistol. She slumped next to him, unconscious.

Beside the table, Keller sank to his knees, his face ashen.

"Secret sauce on the roast?" Kruger asked. Keller said nothing. Even the pallor of approaching death could not keep the
look of defiance off his face.

"Damn you and and your FSE bastards!" Keller hissed. "I
hope you all burn in hell!"

"We probably will," Kruger agreed. "Why don't you go
ahead and make our reservations?"

He slowly brought the Makarov pistol up and fired one
round into Keller's face. The innkeeper fell over backward,
the back of his head a shattered, bloody mass.

Müeller and the others burst in, their weapons at the ready.
They stopped when they saw Keller dead on the flood.

"What happened?" Müeller asked.

"Don't eat the roast," Kruger advised. "It's tough." He tipped the poisoned platter off onto the floor. The metal platter rang like a bell as it rolled across the floor, coming to rest against the dead man. Kruger pulled Ulle's unconscious form out of her chair and threw her limp body over his shoulder. The jostling brought her around a little, and she began to moan as Kruger started out of the dining room with her.

"If you need me," Kruger said casually over his shoulder, "I'll be upstairs."

Bert Hansen set the phone back in its cradle. The plans were set now. The aircraft would take off an hour after sunset. The four Americans would parachute in before dawn, landing in a field near the coast.

He had gotten the call from the king early this morning. The message told him two things: Shatterhand was still alive and Butakov and his men were dead. Hansen had followed the king's orders, hoping that Butakov had died quickly before he could reveal the identity of his contact in London. So far, there had been no cause for alarm.

Hansen looked at his watch. It was just after ten. Hansen picked up the note pad on which he had written the flight information. He walked out of his tiny office toward the door. His secretary, Sheila, looked up as he passed.

"I'm going to pop over to the chemist's shop," he said as she looked up. "Can I bring you anything?"

"No, thanks," she said returning his smile. "Will you be back before lunch?"

"Absolutely!" he called over his shoulder as the door shut behind him.

He walked the two blocks to the car park and retrieved the Rover. Twenty minutes later, he was on the motorway out of London.

It was nearly eleven when he reached the safehouse. There was no sign of life around the house, no tire tracks in the drive. The house had not been compromised. He pulled up in front and quickly went in, making for the door that led to the basement stairs.

It took a minute to look up the frequency for the day and dial it in to the large, single side band radio. Another twenty minutes was lost encoding the message.

When he was finally ready, Hansen switched on the transmitter and fed in the message that began: Rodina, this is Spartacus. He sent the message twice, then waited for an acknowledgement. It was quick in coming. Hansen shut off the radio and went back up into the house.

He was happy to find that Butakov's butchers had left some gin in the pantry. They had cleaned out all the whiskey. He took a long swig from the bottle, feeling the fiery liquid burn its way down his throat. So far, so good. Butakov had failed, but he was still alive, still a trusted aide to the king.

Perhaps I'll give Sheila a tumble tonight, he thought as he left the house; it'll settle my nerves. With that cheerful thought, he drove back to London, whistling as he went.

NINE

"Did I mention that I hate jumping out of airplanes?" Kinski whined above the roar of the old de Havilland's engine.

"Only about a thousand times!" Mamudi groaned as he popped out the eye with the Navy SEAL emblem on it and replaced it with a lighter fiberglass globe painted a flat black. The black eye, combined with the long jagged scar on his face, made the Afghan look like a mutant warrior from some distant world.

They had been flying for hours, winding their way across Europe toward the coordinates provided by the anonymous broadcasters.

"Who do you think sent those radio messages?" Kinski asked.

"Either some of Maximov's enemies," Chan replied, "or one of his own radio operators."

"We'll find out in a minute," Jack Keenan said above the roar. "Get ready, we're six minutes out."

The four men unhooked their yellow nylon static lines and clipped them into metal rings on the de Havilland's flat floor. The copilot came back and opened the side door, strapping it against the back bulkhead. He moved to the other side of the cargo bay as Keenan moved into the door.

"Any one going to be there to meet us?" Kinski asked.

"If there are," Keenan answered, "they aren't going to be friendly!"

The red jump light came on beside the door, indicating that they were only a minute from the drop zone.

The four men checked their equipment one last time, pulled their goggles down into place, and crowded around the open door. A few seconds later, the red light turned to green. Keenan led the way, stepping out into the prop blast, his arms and legs out to stabilize him in the thin air at 10,000 feet. Kinski followed, his protests now forgotten. Mamudi was next. Buddha Chan was the last one out. When the four men had vanished into the dark sky outside, the copilot pulled in the expended deployment bags and replaced the jump door. The de Havilland flew on for twenty more minutes, then turned for home.

"I hear them!" Poulus said, pointing to the western sky. Kruger rubbed his arms again with his hands. The droning engine was clearly audible in the still night.

Kruger had been thinking about Müeller. The silly bastard had been so surprised! He had really believed that he would get rich after turning over the missiles. Kruger had lured him into the car by promising a party with real champagne and willing blond girls.

He had driven Müeller to a remote lake cabin. The silly man had jumped out of the car yelling for girls and wine. Müeller's confused stare had amused him no end. The dupe had pleaded and cried, begged for his life. Kruger had let him. Somehow, the begging and crying made the killing even more satisfying. He had shot Müeller in both knees first, then the shoulders. Müeller had fallen over on his side then, unable to get up, but still able to beg for his life.

Kruger then shot him in the belly. Müeller doubled up in pain and Kruger watched him writhe for a moment before shooting him once in the side of the head. It had been a very satisfying night.

Thinking of Müeller's pleading reminded him of Ulle. She had amused him most of the last night they had been on the coast. The successful recovery of the missiles, Ulle, Müeller, and Maximov's praise had made the last month very special.

Now I'll bag these bastards, he thought, and I'll be set for life.

The plane was nearly overhead now. Poulus was watching it through an old night vision scope.

"They're out, I think," Poulus said. "Four of them."

Kruger looked at his watch. "Right on time!" he observed.

The canopies had deployed perfectly. Now they drifted through the dark sky like four flying mattresses. The four jumpers moved into a loose diamond formation as they flew their airfoil parachutes toward the small clearing that had been selected as their drop zone. The clearing was about five kilometers from the coordinates given in the radio messages. They would walk those kilometers on the ground. It would take several minutes to drift down to the clearing. Kinski, Mamudi and Chan watched Keenan. He led the way.

A thousand feet above the ground, Keenan pulled the straps that held the big pack under his emergency chute. The pack fell fifteen feet to the end of its lowering line. In two more minutes they would be back on the ground in Germany.

"Get ready!" Kruger hissed into the small radio.

"Group One, ready."

"Group Two, ready."

Kruger's force waited in the darkness for the four Americans. He had nearly a hundred of the FSE's best soldiers with him. Tonight, he would pull four thorns from the chairman's side.

The parachutists were nearly to the treetops now, their parachutes silently gliding into the flat clearing. When the first dangling pack hit the ground, Kruger pressed the transmit button on his radio.

"FIRE!" he screamed. "FIRE!"

The edge of the field lit up with yellow flashes that looked like flaming fireflies. The loud muzzle blasts followed a second later.

The four men disappeared into the tall grass in the clearing.

"Move in and get them!" Kruger barked into the radio. The two other groups fanned out and slowly began to sweep the field. They would drive the Americans to him.

"Holy shit!" Kinski yelled as the first bursts whined by overhead. The bullets sounded like angry bees seeking them out.

He was struggling to free his weapon when his rucksack hit the ground below him. He straightened up, flared out the chute and lightly touched down, diving into a forward roll to take cover in the grass. In a moment, he had his weapon free. As he reached for his pack, a fusillade ripped through his gear, rolling it along in the grass. Kinski rolled away from the pack as more slugs ripped through the grass, seeking to rip his body as well.

He rolled into a crouch and ran toward the sound of an American M14 that boomed out a few meters away. Buddha Chan was already in action.

"Don't shoot, Buddha," Kinski called as he burst through the grass next to his friend.

"Shut the fuck up and help me here," Chan snarled. "We got suckered, Bud!" Chan was lying behind his rucksack, popping one round after another into the darkness, aiming at the muzzle flashes. Screams from the dark tree line indicated his hits.

To the right, more shooting broke out. A lone M16 answered a chorus of AK's. At least one of the Marauders was still alive there. Kinski knelt and began firing short bursts at a group of dark shapes that had detached themselves from the tree line. One figure after another fell, but more came on, closing the distance in the darkness. Ten short bursts later, his magazine was empty.

"Buddha," he whispered, "Let's move it! These bastards are on us like ducks on a June bug!"

"I'm right in front of you," Chan answered, rising to a crouch and shouldering the heavy pack. "Let's boogie!" He trotted off into the darkness toward the shooting on the far end of the drop zone, his M14 in front of him. Kinski followed.

Ahead of them, the firing was sporadic. Keenan and Mamudi were still in the fight, but the volume of fire was dropping off. A moment later, it stopped altogether. Kinski and Chan stopped to listen for any signs of their two friends.

Behind them, a flare arced up into the sky, lighting the area with an eerie, flickering blue-white light.

"These fuckers knew we were coming!" Chan hissed, "they were waiting for us!" The silence ahead of them was depressing. If Keenan and Mamudi were still alive, they would be firing. The quiet meant that they were surely dead.

"Come on, Ace," Chan snarled, "we need to un-ass this kill zone." He turned and jogged off across the clearing, heading for the far tree line. Kinski. followed, heartsick and angry.

As he trotted along behind Chan, Kinski suddenly spun to the ground. Pain like a hot ice pick stabbed up his left arm.

"Buddha, I'm hit!" Kinski gasped. Kinski felt his short friend's hands under his armpits. Chan jerked him to his feet, causing the ice pick in his arm to become a pickax. He grit his teeth as Chan put a thick arm around him and pulled him along.

"I hate it when this happens!" Kinski hissed as the two remaining Marauders made their way out of what had become a drop zone of death.

Kruger's radio crackled again.

"Group One," the voice rasped, strained with tension, "we have been hit hard. Two Americans shot their way through us. We are pursuing them."

"Shit!" Kruger swore. "Group Two, Report."

There was no answer. He tried again. Again there was no answer.

What are these men? Kruger wondered. They hit like sledge-hammers, then slip through your fingers like quicksilver. He had heard rumors of genetic experiments before the Nuke-Out, maybe these Marauders were the result of those experiments.

"Come on, Poulus," Kruger barked. "Our rats are slipping through the trap. Put the men on line, we're going to flush them out ourselves."

"Damn it!" Keenan cursed as the firing behind them slowed, then stopped. He could hear the voices of their pursuers, the grass and branches breaking beneath their feet. The adrenalin rush on the drop zone had kicked his enhanced senses up all the way. Now he felt like he was buzzing all over.

Keenan was ignoring the waves of smell that assaulted his nose. The clean, wet smell of the grass, the musty smell of the dirt that clung to their boots, the pungent smell of pine resin all fought for olfactory dominance.

His mouth tasted like he had been sucking on a new penny for a week. Next to him, Mamudi was breathing hard. Keenan could feel the anger and despair that radiated from the Afghan.

"Jack," Mamudi whispered, "can you tell if they're alive? Can you sense them?"

"No," the furious giant hissed, "I can't tell." He frowned at Mamudi in the darkness. "I don't think they made it."

The deep sigh that escaped from Mamudi's lips said volumes. "Come on, Jack," Mamudi urged. "We cannot avenge them if we do not live ourselves."

Keenan closed his eyes and searched with his mind for any trace of his missing friends. There was too much static, both from the enemy in the clearing and inside his own head from the anger and frustration of their betrayal. He could not find Kinski or Chan at all.

Mamudi pulled at his combat harness. Keenan allowed himself to be pulled away from the ambush. Freddie was right. He couldn't make the bastards pay for Chan and Kinski with blood if he was not alive. And pay they would, at an exchange rate of a hundred to one. Keenan would see to that.

Donovan burst into the king's office.

"Your Grace," he blurted as Shatterhand and the group of Ministers looked up in surprise, "I'm sorry to interrupt, but we have intercepted a message!" He stood panting, holding a piece of yellow note pad in front of him.

Shatterhand took the paper. "What is it?" he asked the signals officer.

"It's a message to Maximov," Donovan went on, as a low murmur rose from the group of ministers. "I believe that it is about the Marauders."

"Who sent it?" Shatterhand asked, suddenly concerned.

"Don't know yet, Your Grace," Donovan admitted, "It was sent from somewhere outside London, but we didn't get a good fix on the transmitter."

"Damn," the king said, looking at the big grandfather clock that stood at one end of the large room.

"Is it too late to stop them?" Shatterhand asked.

"Yes, sir, much too late," Donovan admitted.

"Then they're doomed," Shatterhand speculated. One of the ministers interrupted.

"We've thought that they were doomed before, Your Grace," he observed.

"I hope we're wrong this time, too," Shatterhand agreed. He turned back to McMillan, the Special Branch man.

"Find out who sent this," he instructed. "I want this leak plugged."

"Yes, Your Grace," McMillan answered. He rose and accompanied Donovan from the room.

"They're in God's hands now," one of the other ministers observed.

Shatterhand laughed. "I think God has been keeping his distance from those men for some time now!"

The assembled ministers laughed as the king rejoined the meeting.

TEN

He could still hear them. They were close.

Not close enough to get a shot at them, but close enough to keep the two of them running until they dropped.

"Jack," Mamudi urged his breath ragged from running all night, "let's fight them. We haven't ever run from a fight, let's not start now."

Crazy Jack Keenan dropped to the damp ground and rubbed his face with his hand. "You're right, Freddie," the red-haired giant agreed. "That fuck-up on the DZ spooked me." Keenan looked back toward the clearing where Maximov's thugs had been waiting for them.

"Somebody gave our butts up, that's for sure, but that doesn't mean we have to roll over." Keenan checked his M16. He had half a magazine left in the weapon and two more in his ammo pouch, for a total of seventy-five rounds.

"How much ammo you got?" he asked Mamudi.

"Two full magazines," the wiry SEAL replied, "and a grenade."

"Well, one thing for sure," Keenan observed, "it won't be a real long fight."

"Perhaps," Mamudi suggested, "as Chairman Mao said in his Red Book, we can shoot one and scare a thousand."

"I'd rather shoot a thousand and scare all the rest of 'em!" Keenan answered. The wild, wolfish smile Mamudi knew so well returned to Keenan's face. "Come on, Freddie," he said punching Mamudi's shoulder, "there's two of us left, we'll surround them!"

They were close, now. Kruger could almost smell them.

"Commander," Poulus panted as he caught Kruger's sleeve, "we need to be careful." The man's words came in rushes, forced out between gasps. "We're getting strung out and separated in these woods. I'm afraid of an ambush!" Poulus called Kruger commander in the field. No one knew Kruger's military rank, or even if he had any rank, but everyone knew that Kruger was Chairman Maximov's hatchet man. He seemed to like being a Commander, so Poulus always called him that.

"And I'm afraid they'll get away!" Kruger snapped at his exhausted subordinate. "Don't quit on me now," Kruger warned. "We are close to catching them. I can smell them just up ahead."

Behind them, the sixty survivors of last night's action stumbled along in pursuit of the American parachutists. The four Americans had killed or wounded the other forty.

The ground was rising now. The forest, devoid of any underbrush, was dotted now and then by large boulders. Kruger moved a bit farther back behind the line of searchers. There were sometimes snakes behind rocks. Better to let one of the troops get bitten first. This morning, the memory of those forty soldiers was still vivid.

Ten minutes later, his fears were validated. The ragged staccato of gunfire broke out ahead. In the first second, nearly a dozen of his men fell writhing to the ground, ripped by fire from—where?

Poulus came running back from the ambush, his left arm dangling at his side.

"The rocks!" he shouted, pointing back and up with the barrel of his rifle. "They're above us on a bluff!"

"How many?" Kruger barked.

"Two, I think!" Poulus gasped, "I saw the muzzle flashes." He looked down at his bleeding arm. "They're good shots."

Kruger's troops were returning the fire now. "Keep them pinned down," Kruger ordered, "I will go around them."

"Suck on that, Klaus," Keenan muttered as he changed magazines in his M16. Their first burst had taken out a long section of the assault line. Now their pursuers were dispersed into the trees, shooting up the entire cliff face.

"Ready, Freddie?" Keenan called. Mamudi nodded, thumbing the bolt release, slamming a fresh round into his rifle's smoking chamber.

"Hit the road, Jack," Mamudi answered, darting down the thin trail that led down one side of the bluff. With luck, the FSE jerks would waste a lot of time and most of their ammo shooting up the bluff.

By the time they figured out the fight was one sided, the two Marauders would have another ambush set up. They would keep up the hit and run tactic until the FSE gave up or they ran out of targets.

Mamudi was leading the way. He was halfway down the hill when a flurry of shots rang out ahead. The rocks around them chipped and splattered.

"Get back, Jack!" Mamudi suggested as he hastily beat a path back up the trail. The rattle of AK's grew in intensity as Keenan and Mamudi ducked back behind the sheltering rocks atop the bluff.

Behind them, a handful of the bravest of the FSE flankers dashed up the trail, firing wildly, searching for targets.

Mamudi popped up between two boulders and cut down the attackers with a long burst that slammed the men against the rocks, leaving red trails on the granite as they fell into still lumps in the trail.

"I'm open to suggestions," Mamudi said, dropping the empty magazine. He pulled a loaded one from his ammo pouch and slammed it up into the weapon. "I've only got one more magazine."

"We might try prayer," Keenan suggested, "I'll give Jesus a call, you check with Allah."

"Don't blaspheme, Jack!" Mamudi snapped.

"I'm serious, guy," Keenan answered as another burst ripped across the rocks overhead. "I think we've screwed the pooch this time!"

A pair of bold FSEs rushed up the trail. Two rounds from Keenan's rifle cut short the career of one of them. "Lord help me, Jesus," he whispered as he lined up the second one in his sights.

• • •

He had them now. Unless there was another path down from the bluff, the two Marauders were trapped. Now he would take them.

Kruger sent word back to Poulus to send half his men around to Kruger and to keep up a steady fire on the bluff. Poulus would keep their heads down while Kruger and his assault force dug the Americans out. It was just a matter of time. After he killed these two, he would go after the other pair who had escaped from the drop zone.

A few minutes later, the messenger was back with eight of Poulus's men. Kruger placed four two-man fire teams at the face of the bluff to keep up continuous fire support.

"Ready?" he asked the others. They nodded, but Kruger could see they were not eager to take on the men who had killed so many of their comrades. "Let's move!"

The fire support team opened up on the rocks. Kruger motioned for the assault element to move up the trail. Overhead, a loud pop caught Kruger's attention. He looked up to see several small cans falling form a cloud of white smoke overhead.

"What the . . . ?" Kruger asked. One of the little cans hit the rocks above. It exploded with a loud bang.

"Take cover!" he screamed as the other cans dropped all around them. The rocks rang with explosions and the air was filled with whining metal bits that ripped through his assault force. Kruger dove to the ground as bits of metal dug into his right leg.

Overhead, two more pops dropped more of the lethal little bombs all over his troops. Kruger buried himself in the dirt to escape the metal storm that raged around him, screaming as he waited for death.

ELEVEN

"Got any idea where we are?" Kinski asked.

"Germany," Chan answered, searching the open field in front of them with his rifle scope.

"Right," Kinski said. "Thank you for clearing that up!"

They had run all night. Now he and Buddha Chan were holed up in a small copse of trees. Around them, wide meadows stretched in three directions. His arm was throbbing. The wound was clean, through and through, and it had stopped bleeding, but it hurt like hell.

"I feel like shit, man," Kinski said, dabbing his wound with iodine from the first aid packet on his web gear. "We ran out on them!"

Chan looked over at him, his eyes slits behind the yellow glasses.

"We didn't even know where they were," he reminded Kinski, "and we barely shot our way out as it was." He took off the shooters glasses and wiped the lenses. "We survived. Now we can dish out some payback!"

The Mongol sniper cradled his rifle in his lap and leaned against a tree. "I need some Zs, take the first watch."

"Right," Kinski answered. In seconds, Buddha was snoring softly. Kinski sat cross-legged, watching the fields. Exhaustion, guilt and hunger pulled at him. They'd been in tight spots before, but this time Kinski felt a real foreboding. This whole deal sucked bad. His eyes felt heavy. He'd let Buddha sleep a little while, then get some sleep himself. He closed his eyes for a moment to rest them.

When he opened his eyes, Kinski was looking at the largest pair of pale white breasts he had ever seen. They were bulging out of a bright blue dress embroidered with little yellow daisies.

Kinski tore his eyes from the massive knockers and looked up into two cornflower blue eyes framed by wisps of straight yellow hair. For a moment, Kinski thought he had bled to death in his sleep, that this was an angel. The angel took a sudden deep breath that almost set the two creamy mounds free from their restraints and said, "Guten Tag."

Kinski, his back against the tree, tried to back pedal, to escape. His legs, still crossed in front of him, refused to move. In fact, he couldn't feel his legs at all. His arm throbbed though, reminding him of his wound.

"Buddha!" Kinski shouted. "We got company!"

"Thanks for the bulletin, dickhead," Chan answered calmly. "I have been talking to our buxom friend here for half an hour." As Kinski squirmed, the big blonde stood up and Kinski got a better look at her.

She was close to six feet tall, and her big bust and flaring hips framed a tiny waist. Towering above him, she looked more like an angel than ever.

"You went to sleep," Chan observed.

"I know," Kinski admitted. "Sorry."

"Not as sorry as you would have been if Maximov's people had found us instead of Greta here."

"Greta," Kinski said, repeating her name. It had a musical sound. She smiled and her smile seemed to light up the dark glade.

"Ja?" she asked, hearing her name.

"Sprecken sie Anglais?" Kinski asked her, untangling his numb legs.

"Yes," she answered brightly. "A little bit, okay?"

"Great!" he answered. She leaned down again to stare at his face, and once again he could see to China down the bodice of her dark blue dress.

"You look yoost like gear!" she cooed.

Kinski's face wrinkled in confusion. "What kind of gear?" he asked. Behind him Chan snorted.

"Richard Gere," Chan chuckled. "This poor nearsighted girl thinks you look like Richard Gere." Chan shook his head and laughed. Kinski reached for his metal comb and ran it through his badly damaged pompadour. Greta smiled her approval.

"She and her folks live near here," Chan explained. "They hate the FSE. She says we can stay there for a while and regroup."

"What a great idea!" Kinski said enthusiastically. He tried to stand and a thousand pins and needles shot through his cramped legs. Greta reached down, her bountiful breasts swaying hypnotically as she helped him up. Kinski caught a whiff of cheap perfume mixed with sweat, a scent that sent his senses reeling. Behind him, Buddha Chan laughed again.

When the pop went off over them, Mamudi glanced up then slammed them both into the rocks.

"Damn it, Freddie!" Keenan swore, his mouth and nose suddenly filled with dust and bits of rock. A second later, explosions rang off the rocks around them.

"CBUs!" Mamudi shouted over the din. The SEAL grabbed Keenan's BDUs and dragged him backward deeper into the rocks as more pops went off overhead. Below them, the FSE force was being shredded by the rain of small bombs.

The barrage went on for several minutes. When it finally stopped, no more gunfire came from below, only moans and screams from the few survivors at the bottom of the bluff.

"It would seem that our prayers have not gone unheeded," Mamudi observed.

"Come on, babe," Keenan urged, "let's boogie!"

They slipped through the rocks down the now-bloody trail and disappeared into the woods again. An hour later, Keenan called a rest stop on the bank of a wide stream.

"Well, Freddie," Keenan observed, washing his face in the clear, cold water, "I guess we have some allies here after all. Unless God and Allah have a separate artillery section." He motioned for Mamudi's canteen.

"Although they were indeed welcome," Mamudi answered, tossing the green plastic canteen, "I doubt that those rounds were divine."

"What were those things that went off over us, anyway?" Keenan asked as he refilled the water bottles.

"Cluster bomb rounds from a mortar," Mamudi explained. "I saw some experimental ones before the war. They're fired from an 81mm mortar, then they break up over the target and drop a handful of bomblets on the enemy."

"Whatever they were, they did a job on those jokers!" Keenan smiled, tossing back the full canteen.

"I'm trying to remember what they were called," Mamudi said, washing his face with a handful of water from the canteen.

"They are Multiple Munition Mortar Projectiles," an accented voice said from behind the tree that Mamudi was leaning against.

Keenan swept up his rifle and fired a burst that stripped the bark off just above Mamudi's head. Mamudi rolled to one side coming up in a crouch, his M16 in front of him.

"Relax, gentlemen," another voice said from behind Keenan, "we are your friends. We sent the message."

"We fired the mortars that killed the FSEs at the bluff," the first voice concurred.

Keenan and Mamudi exchanged looks. Whoever these guys were, they had the two of them dead to rights.

Why didn't I sense these guys? Keenan wondered, as he stood up and propped the M16 against his hip.

"You guys got names?" he asked the two unseen strangers.

"Indeed," a tall thin man dressed in a Soviet paratrooper smock said as he stepped from behind a thick pine.

"Permit me to introduce us," a shorter, heavyset man in an identical outfit offered as he, too, emerged from behind cover. "I am Senior Sergeant Arkady Kron, 800th Guards Independent Special Purpose Battalion. This officer is Ensign Viktor T'sinko."

"Spetsnaz!" Keenan blurted. "I thought all you guys were dead!"

"Like so many stories about us," T'sinko answered, "the rumors of our destruction were somewhat exaggerated."

Keenan shouldered his rifle and stepped up to T'sinko, who was nearest him. "I don't know how you got here," the red haired giant said, shaking T'sinko's hand, "but you saved our butts. Thanks!"

A feral smile split T'sinko's face. "It is always a pleasure to kill the FSE dogs."

Mamudi eyed the two strangers. Their camouflage smocks blended perfectly with the foliage. The taller man had the lanky, self-assured manner of an athlete. His hair was rough cut, probably by the other man's knife. His expression was casual, almost amused. His pale gray eyes flickered with interest and curiosity.

The other man was a Soviet clone of Buddha Chan. There was nothing casual about him. He looked at the two Americans with undisguised mirth, a wide Cossack smile across his dark face.

These Russians look like a tree and a bush, Mamudi chuckled to himself.

"You sent the message about the missiles?" Mamudi asked their benefactors.

"Just so," Kron answered. "At this moment, they are in the Schloss Adler."

"The who?" Keenan asked.

"The Schloss Adler," T'sinko interrupted. "It is a castle atop a mountain south of here. Maximov's headquarters are there."

Keenan sat on a fallen log. "Well," he said, "we came here to get those missiles, but most of our gear was lost on the DZ. Those goons back there knew we were coming."

"So it would appear," T'sinko agreed, "but we can help you with the equipment." Both Soviets smiled knowingly. "Come, we will show you a place that no one else knows of."

The two Russians turned and walked off through the forest. Keenan and Mamudi looked at each other for a second, then followed, jogging to keep up with the two strange Soviet soldiers.

TWELVE

Greta's family lived on a farm that looked like a picture postcard. The buildings were all whitewashed until they gleamed in the sun and the farmhouse had banks of flowers all around. In post-nuclear Europe, the farm was a sweet reminder of better times.

The Jodl family had owned the farm for generations. Greta was the only child left; the boys had been killed fighting Maximov's goons two years before when the dictator had seized all of Europe and stamped out all opposition to his new reich.

Chan and Kinski were welcomed like liberators. Greta's mom fed them until they were stuffed. After the meal, Greta and her mother tended Kinski's wounded arm while her dad regaled them with stories.

The Jodls wanted them to sleep in the house, but Chan thought it would be better if they slept in the barn. Greta's mom supplied them with quilts and, a little after midnight, they made their way into the loft by candlelight and sacked out on the hay.

Kinski was dead asleep when he was suddenly awakened by a warm, soft hand over his mouth. His eyes flew open and there was Greta's face just above his. She placed her finger over her lips and took her hand away. She was on her knees beside him and even in the dark barn, he could see the pale whiteness of her breasts against the dark fabric of her dress.

She stood and motioned for him to follow and bring the quilt. She led him out of the barn to a workshop attached to the barn's outside wall. It was dark in the workshop, but Greta took the quilt and spread it on the floor. She pulled Kinski down onto the quilt.

"You are so much pretty!" she whispered as she pulled him close and pressed her full lips to his. Her eager tongue slipped into his mouth and Kinski felt the warmth of her breasts through his shirt.

She pushed him onto his back and moved over him, never breaking the searing kiss. Kinski's pulse was racing. Greta had splashed more of her dime store perfume on and its heavy floral scent filled his head as she bent over him. "Yoost like Richard Gere!" she giggled.

Kinski thought for a fleeting second about the real Richard Gere. The handsome actor was undoubtedly a small pile of radioactive ashes mixed with the ashes of everyone else in Hollywood. Los Angeles had been hit by several nukes at once.

"Thank you, Richard, wherever you are," Kinski whispered as he pushed his fingers under the elastic bodice of Greta's dress and pushed it toward her feet. Her bodacious ta-tas spilled from the dress and orbited hypnotically just above Kinski's bare chest.

Greta lowered her massive mammaries onto him and dragged them slowly back and forth across his chest as she raised mouth-to-mouth resuscitation to an art form. Finally she broke the kiss and whispered sweet German nothings in his ear, biting as she spoke.

"Here, miene hero," she breathed, pulling one big breast up to his face. Kinski sucked eagerly on the hard nipple.

If this isn't heaven, he thought, it'll do for now.

When he stumbled back up into the loft an hour later, Chan was sitting up, leaning against the wall, smoking a cigarette.

"Well, well," he said sarcastically, "look who's back. So how was the Teutonic Titwillow? Did she hurt your arm?"

"Eat your heart out, buddy," Kinski said, collapsing onto the damp quilt. In seconds, Kinski was sleeping. Chan finished his smoke, chuckled as he snubbed it out, and curled up on his warm quilt.

Kinski, you lucky bastard, he thought as he, too, dropped off to sleep again.

"What do you mean they got away?" Maximov shouted into the phone. "How could they get away?" He tapped a pencil on the polished desk as he listened to Kruger, down at the lower garrison, as he explained his failure to kill or capture the four Americans. Kruger had been brought back by the survivors of his ambush force. He was wounded, but not too seriously.

"Kruger," Maximov hissed, "I want you to take Captain Pilski's company and find those men! Don't come back until you find them!" He listened again. "That's right, my friend. Come back with your shield or on it, Kruger," he barked. "I'll have their heads or yours!"

He hung up the phone and broke the pencil out of irritation.

Dawn was a pale gray line on the horizon when the two Russians finally stopped.

"We are here," T'sinko said matter-of-factly.

Keenan and Mamudi looked around in the dim light. They appeared to be in a clearing about forty meters wide. There was no sign of any camp or anything else.

"Here? Where?" Keenan asked.

T'sinko smiled and stepped over to a thick bush on one side of the clearing. He reached into the bush and pulled out a padlock that held a chain together. He reached into his smock and pulled out a small key. Unlocking the padlock, he reached into the bush and pulled. A huge section of the bush moved forward. T'sinko motioned them to follow, then stepped into the moveable hedge.

Keenan and Mamudi followed the Russian. The foliage was only a few meters thick. When they emerged on the other side, they were facing a metal door set into the rock wall of a small hill.

"Alice through the looking glass," Mamudi said as T'sinko spun the dial of a combination lock on the door and pushed down on a steel lever beneath the lock.

The door swung open and T'sinko went in. Behind them, Kron was pulling the foliage shut.

Inside the door was a short hallway that led to another door. A row of tiny lights in the ceiling gave off just enough light to navigate the hall. Beyond the door, bright fluorescent light lit a large room. As Keenan and Mamudi entered, their mouths dropped open.

Inside the big room were several wire-mesh enclosed compartments. Through the mesh, the two Marauders could see racks of weapons and equipment.

"I know what some of this stuff is," Mamudi said, "but I've never even seen a bunch of it!"

"What is this place, Victor?" Keenan asked T'sinko.

The Russian was shuffling off his pack. It fell to the floor with a loud metallic clank.

"It was a NATO experimental weapons test facility," T'sinko answered, opening the pack and pulling out the mortar tube that protruded from the top. He laid it on the floor and pulled out the bipod, too.

"How did you find it?" Mamudi asked, "It must have been classified."

"It was our target," Kron answered as he walked up behind them. He hefted the big pack off his back, pulled the round aluminum mortar baseplate out and set it next to the tube. "We knew all about it," he went on. "When the balloon went up, we came to take the place out."

T'sinko took up the narrative. "Before we could attack, the nukes went off. The people who worked here didn't come back, so instead of destroying it, we moved in."

"Come on," he offered, "I will show you around." He led the two amazed Americans past the wire enclosures. Inside them, all manner of futuristic hardware gleamed. Past the wire enclosures was a tunnel that went further back into the hill.

"The labs and tech rooms are down there," T'sinko explained as they passed the tunnel and entered a stairwell leading down. Downstairs, they emerged into a large circular room. Long tunnels extended out from the room like spokes from a hub.

"These are the test ranges," T'sinko went on. "Outside, you can't hear anything."

"And NATO just walked away and left all this?" Keenan asked incredulously.

A bemused smile crossed T'sinko's face. "Perhaps they felt it was superfluous, everything considered."

Keenan stood shaking his head. Mamudi was silent, reflecting on the past.

Once I would have killed this man on sight, he mused, looking at their enigmatic host. Today he saved my life and I find that I like him.

"All soldiers are brothers," he said aloud. Keenan and T'sinko turned to look at him. "Sorry," Mamudi apologized, "just thinking aloud." For a second, Mamudi thought he saw T'sinko's face change, a look of understanding flickering across his chiseled features.

"Come, my friends," the Russian said, turning for the stairs. "You will need some new equipment."

"We need a whole new plan," Keenan answered miserably.

"Perhaps we can help you with that, too."

Upstairs, the smell of food caught their attention. It suddenly dawned on Keenan how hungry he was. Kron had four plastic bags of food set out on a long metal table.

"MREs!" Keenan exclaimed, "God, I feel like I'm in a museum here!"

"They also tested clothing and equipment here," Kron explained. "Food, too."

The four sat down in folding metal chairs and devoured the hot food. No one spoke for several minutes as they stuffed their faces with the entrees.

As he ate, Keenan wondered. He hadn't sensed the two Russians at all nor smelled the food until they were in the same room. Had the neurotoxin finally worn off? For a second, Keenan felt like an amputee, missing a limb.

As he worried about the loss of his heightened senses, the smell of the hot beans and franks suddenly assaulted his nose. The food in his mouth began to play his taste buds like a lingual pinball. The sound of the other men's plastic spoons scraping on the plastic food bags sounded like shovels mixing concrete in a wheelbarrow.

Keenan laughed out loud. When the others looked at him, he smiled and said, "I'm back!" The others looked at Crazy Jack like he was indeed a madman, then quickly went back to their food.

When all the plastic bags were empty, T'sinko stood and stretched. "Get some sleep, gentlemen," he suggested. "Later we will pick out some new toys for you to play with, eh?"

"We gotta get outta here," Chan said between bites. "We still got a mission, even if there's only two of us."

"I personally want to find the bastard that bushwhacked us on the DZ," Kinski blurted, sending bits of egg and bratwurst flying.

"First, we find those friggen' missiles!" Chan insisted. "Then we'll kick his ass!"

A day's rest had restored their customary confidence. Now both men were eager to avenge the killing of their teammates. Kinski's wound was healing and he was trying hard to ignore it altogether.

"Got any idea where to look?" Kinski asked.

"I figure wherever the FSE bigwigs are, that's where we'll find the missiles," Chan answered. "Maybe the Jodls know where their HQ is."

"We'll need more firepower than these," Kinski complained, thumping the black plastic stock of his M16.

"We'll borrow some from the FSE!" Chan said, smiling grimly.

A clattering on the loft ladder made both men reach for their weapons. Greta's pretty face appeared above the edge.

"You are finished eating?" she asked brightly.

"Seeing you makes me hungry again!" Kinski replied. She blushed furiously, her pale cheeks and chest reddening.

"Come on, Buddha," Kinski said, never taking his eyes from his blushing Valkyrie. "Let's see what Greta's folks know." They followed her down the ladder and over to her house. Greta was still blushing when they went into the immaculate house.

"Herr Jodl," Chan asked, "where is the FSE's main headquarters around here?"

Jodl looked to the south, an angry expression setting the deep lines in his weathered face. "Schloss Adler," he answered, pointing south, "an old fortress atop a steep mountain. The main force is quartered around the base of the mountain, but the headquarters is up in the castle."

He took a scrap of paper and drew a crude sketch. "The only way to reach the castle is a cable car that runs up to the castle from the village across the river. Maximov has a small fort around the cable car terminal to guard it." He leaned back for the two Americans to see.

Kinski whistled through his teeth. "Shee-it," he observed. He looked up quickly. "Sorry, Frau Jodl." Greta giggled.

"Would you know how large this fortress is?" Chan asked.

"Oh, yes," Jodl replied. "I've been there several times. Before." He looked sad for just a second, then the sadness was replaced by anger. "The fortress is bounded by a wall. Inside the wall, there is a space as large as a soccer field, maybe larger."

"Plenty of room for a couple of crummy cruise missiles," Chan observed. Kinski nodded. They started for the door.

"We need more weapons to take on a castle," Kinski said, "We'll be back for dinner. If we're still welcome."

"You are always welcome here," Jodl answered. Greta blushed again in agreement. Kinski winked at her and the two men disappeared out the door.

"What the hell is this thing?" Keenan asked as he hefted the green plastic rifle. It appeared to be a seamless green box. The only opening was the tiny one at the muzzle and a larger one below.

"It's an H&K G-11," T'sinko explained, "4.7mm."

"Where does the ammo go?" Keenan asked turning the weapon over.

T'sinko pressed a catch on top of the weapon. The entire top front of the weapon detached into his hand. "This whole thing is the magazine," he explained. "It holds 50 rounds."

"Radical," Keenan said shaking his head. "Where does the empty brass eject? There's no ejection port."

"There is no brass," T'sinko went on. "The bullet is encased in the propellant."

Keenan shook his head. The German rifle made his M16 look like a club with a nail in it by comparison. Under the tiny rifle muzzle, the wide snout of a grenade launcher gaped.

"The grenade launcher takes the standard 40mm high explosive and white phosphorus rounds," his Spetsnaz instructor explained, pressing the rubberized nub that let the grenade launcher barrel go forward to receive a grenade.

"How much ammo you got for these babies?" Keenan asked.

T'sinko smiled. "Several cases! There is an ammunition bunker downstairs as well."

Keenan smiled at his Russian host. "There's plenty of stuff here to kick Maximov's ass with. Will you help us?"

"We have been helping you all along, my friend," T'sinko replied. A strange look came over the tall man. "Ever since this gangster, this *chekist*, proclaimed himself ruler of his Federated States," T'sinko spat, his eyes flashing, "we have tormented his men around here. We snipe at his patrols and disrupt his communications." A sadder look darkened the Russian's face. "We would do more, but there have been reprisals against the civilians after our raids. We do not wish to kill innocents by our actions."

"We've seen his goons at work," Keenan nodded. "Maximov recruits the scum of the earth."

"Keenan," T'sinko said, "we cannot let Maximov possess these weapons of mass destruction. We will not let him use Soviet nuclear weapons to blackmail the world. It is our duty as Soviet soldiers to prevent it."

Their serious conversation was interrupted by Kron and Mamudi, who returned from a tour of the labs.

"Jack!" Mamudi exclaimed. "You should see the stuff back in there. It's like Six Flags Over Destruction!"

"There is something else, my friends," Kron interrupted. "While Mamudi was examining our toys, I intercepted a message on the FSE frequency. It seems your friends may yet be alive."

Both Americans were immediately in Kron's face.

"How? What did they say?" Keenan demanded, grabbing Kron's smock. "Tell me!"

"Easy, *tovarish*, easy," Kron admonished. "The message was from FSE headquarters to a field unit. They are still looking for all four of you. That means that they have not found your companions, dead or alive."

Keenan whirled and jerked the G-11 from the rack. "Then let's let 'em find a couple of Marauders!" he snarled. "I want to give this baby a workout!"

The two Russians smiled. "It would be our pleasure to accompany you, if you would permit us," Kron suggested.

Keenan tossed Kron the green plastic rifle. "It's your football, the least we can do is let you play!"

T'sinko laughed. "Come, then. We have much to do."

As the two Russians began dragging weapons and magazines out of the wire enclosure, Keenan took Mamudi's sleeve.

"They're alive, Freddie," Keenan said. "We'll find 'em!"

"I never thought otherwise, my friend," the wiry Afghan smiled. "I never thought otherwise!"

THIRTEEN

The little farm looked like a prewar postcard through his binoculars.

"There is no other farm in this area?" Kruger asked Poulus.

"None," Poulus answered. "There is no other place they could have sought refuge."

"Let's go talk to them," Kruger smiled. Kruger's right arm and leg were better now. The shrapnel bits had hurt like hell, but nothing vital had been hit. He was luckier than most of his troops had been. The little bombs had ripped most of them to shreds. The rest had been either wounded or so terrified that they were useless.

Worst of all, the Americans had escaped—again.

If I hadn't been wounded, he thought as they mounted the trucks, Maximov would have executed me himself.

If he blew this attempt, even his wounds might not save him.

There was no activity on the farm; at least none they could see. Kruger's two truckloads of soldiers swept into the farm-yard and skidded to a stop. The troops fanned out quickly, unwilling to be caught in the trucks if the Americans were there. They dispersed to the various buildings, searching each one for the fugitives.

Kruger took Poulus and a squad into the white farmhouse. Inside, an older woman stood terrified in the house's large kitchen.

"Guten Tag, Frau," Kruger asked, his voice very casual and friendly. "Where are the others?"

"There are no others," she stammered. "Only my husband. He is working in the fields!"

"Only your husband?" Kruger asked incredulously, taking a hot biscuit from the basket on the table. "No big strapping sons to work the farm? No hired hands?"

The old woman stiffened. "Both my sons are dead," she said flatly. "We have no money to hire any help."

"How unfortunate!" Kruger sympathized. "But surely the two of you cannot do it all yourself?"

"We manage," she replied. She stood stiffly by the flat lump of dough rolled out on the cabinet.

From the back of the house, a loud scream intruded on their conversation. There was the sound of scuffling and a moment later, two soldiers holding a struggling girl between them entered the kitchen.

Kruger looked the girl over. She was tall and pretty, even though her face was contorted by fear and anger. Her struggling only emphasized her massive bust, straining against her dress as she tried to break the iron grip on her wrists.

"Well," Kruger crooned, "what have we here?" He stepped up to the girl and smiled. "What is your name, pretty one?" he asked. She responded by spitting at him.

Kruger ducked the spit, laughing. He turned to the old woman.

"I thought there were no others?" he asked softly. The old woman's face set like concrete, her eyes looking at some spot miles away. Kruger looked back at the girl then turned and backhanded the old woman. She fell backward, grasping at the counter to keep from falling. She slumped down against the cabinet, her hand stanching the blood that now trickled from the corner of her mouth.

He turned back to the girl. "Perhaps you can tell me how many people live here and where they all are?"

"I will tell you nothing, pigs!" she shouted. Kruger stood watching her, his eyebrows raised.

"Really?" he asked. He pulled his pistol from its holster, turned and fired. The pistol shot roared, stabbing everyone's ears with the blast. The cabinet above the old woman's head splintered.

"No!" the girl screamed. "Please! I'll tell you what you want to know! Don't hurt my mother!" Tears ran down her cheeks, now red from struggling. "The three of us live here," she went on. "My father, mother, and me."

Kruger nodded. "That is better," he said soothingly. "Now I want to ask about some strangers. They are Americans." He watched the girl's face closely. "There are two of them. One may be wounded."

Though she tried to hide it, Kruger could see the flicker of fear that passed over her face at the mention of the two Americans.

Ah, he thought, pay-dirt.

"What is your name, Liebling?" he asked the girl, wiping a tear from her soft cheek. At his touch, she stiffened, pulling her face away.

"Greta," she replied softly, "Greta Jodl."

"Well, Greta," Kruger consoled her, "we do not seek to harm your family!" He put on a mask of compassion. "We know that you and your family are loyal supporters of the Federation! We seek only the Federation's enemies!" He motioned for the two soldiers to release her.

When her arms were freed, the girl dropped to the floor to cradle her mother in her arms. The two women glared at Kruger and his men.

"I know the two Americans were here," Kruger lied. "I know that they forced you to feed them and treat the wounded man. That was not your fault." Kruger pulled out a chair from the small kitchen table and straddled it.

"I only want to know when they left and where they were going." He took another biscuit. Just for a second, Kruger was transported back to his youth, to his mother's kitchen. Her biscuits had smelled just this way. He smiled for a moment at that pleasant memory, then looked back at the two women cowering before him. The old woman's face looked like steel, but the young one lacked her strength.

"Tell me about the Americans," he said. "We will leave you in peace then."

"I don't believe it!" Kinski screamed.

The Jodl farm, so perfect and picturesque just hours ago, was now a smoking wreck. In the barn yard, nearly obscured by smoke, soldiers were climbing into two FSE trucks.

"Bastards!" Chan cursed. This happened so often. Anyone who aided them stood to be tortured or killed, their property destroyed, yet there were always people who insisted on helping them fight against oppression.

"Come on!" Kinski insisted. "We've got to help them!"

"We're too late to help them," Chan replied. "But we're not too late to punish those fuckers!" He pointed down the hill toward the road. "We'll wait for them down there!"

They scrambled down the hill and took up positions fifty yards apart in the trees next to the road. A moment later, they heard the sound of the two trucks.

Poulus, driving the lead truck, glanced over at his boss. Kruger was sitting there with his eyes closed, a disturbing smile on his lips. For his part, Poulus felt sick to his stomach. He was used to brutality and abuse, but Kruger, he was really sick. What he had done to that old woman still made Poulus shiver.

It had worked, though. The girl had talked like a magpie. They would hide the trucks and surround the farm. The Americans would come back to look for the women. When they did, they would die. They would leave the trucks a mile up the road, then walk back to the farm.

Poulus's musings were interrupted by a 109 grain, 5.56mm bullet that entered the side of his head just behind his left eye. The impact blew both Poulus's eyes out of their sockets and for a brief second he looked down at his own lap before he died and fell over against Kruger.

Poulus was dead before Kruger realized what was happening. The rattle of automatic weapons fire was suddenly loud outside the truck.

Kruger grabbed the wheel, pushing dead Poulus against the driver's door. Using the dead man for a shield, Kruger reached over with his foot and jammed the gas pedal down hard.

The old truck lurched forward. Behind him, Kruger could hear screaming and wood splintering as the torrent of steel raked the poor bastards in the truck's open bed. One or two tried to shoot back, but failed.

Kruger slid over, jamming himself against Poulus. He felt more slugs hit the dead man, jolting the still-warm corpse.

"Thank you, my friend," Kruger told the dead man, whose

eyeballs jiggled and danced on their optic-nerve tethers. "I will remember this gracious gesture!"

Two shots tore through the truck cab inches from his head. Kruger hunkered down in the seat and drove as if the "hounds of hell" were behind him, which, in a manner of speaking, they were.

The lead truck was right in front of him when he fired. Kinski led the driver by a nose, then hit him with a single head shot. The troops in the back of the truck snapped their heads around, looking for the source of the fire. Kinski flipped the selector to automatic and raked the bench seats with two long bursts. Dying FSE bodies tumbled out the back of the truck, soaking the dusty road with their blood.

The truck kept going. Kinski popped another burst into the cab to no effect. He dropped the empty magazine and jammed another in. He fired another quick burst at the cab as the truck disappeared in a cloud of dust.

The second truck had not fared as well. The dead driver had hunched forward over the wheel. The truck slowed, then lurched to a stop. Buddha Chan was killing FSE soldiers as fast as he could pull the trigger. A few were rolling over the truck sides.

Kinski put one short burst after another into the fleeing victims. In seconds, the truck was surrounded by twitching, leaking bodies. The two Marauders stepped onto the road and checked each body. None needed a final send-off.

Kinski pulled the driver out of the cab as Chan dragged the dead away from the truck.

"Let's go check out the farm," Kinski said as Chan climbed in beside him.

"You sure you want to?" Chan asked. "It won't be pretty."

"It never is," Kinski answered wearily. "It never was."

They had gone back to the Jodl's farm. The house was burned completely. There was no sign of Greta or her mother. The barn was burned, too.

"Fuckin' low-life, scum-sucking, dip-wad, slime-worm mother-er jumpers!" Chan cursed. He sat on the riddled tailgate of the truck, hanging his head in despair. "Wonder where old man Jodl was when they hit?"

Kinski shook his head. "I hope he wasn't here," he said, looking at the smoldering ruin of the Jodl's farm house.

"I don't know," Chan countered. "It almost might be better if he was."

The two Americans climbed back into the truck and drove off.

"So what do you want to do now?" Kinski asked.

"Find more of the bastards," Chan suggested, "and kill the hell out of them."

FOURTEEN

"If they're alive," Mamudi pondered, "how do we find them? The FSE hasn't had much luck."

"On the contrary," T'sinko contradicted, "the FSE seems to have had entirely too much luck finding them!"

"We'll find 'em," Keenan assured his friend. "I think I'll be able to track 'em down."

"You seem to trust to luck a great deal, Keenan," Kron observed, "or is it intuition?"

Keenan smiled. "Call it a gift."

"If they are actually in the area that the FSE is searching," T'sinko speculated, "they will likely try to acquire more weapons and ammunition. There are only a few small garrisons in that area. I believe we can forecast their probable targets."

He pulled a map of the area over and pointed to half a dozen locations marked by red triangles.

"These are the garrisons," he explained, "I do not think that two men, even two exceptional men, would assault a garrison head-on. In their place, I, or rather we, would ambush a column." All heads nodded in agreement.

Kron took over. "The best ambush sites are here"—he pointed to an area near the Schloss Adler—"and here. Of the two, this one is nearer their last known area, and farthest from reinforcement. I suggest we watch this area. Your friends may well show up there."

• • •

"Ready?"

"Bring 'em on!" Chan grinned.

"I wish we had more firepower than this one RPG," Kinski complained. "At least we have plenty of ammo for these AKs."

The sound of engines stirred the still air. The sun was high overhead. Chan hefted the RPG onto his shoulder. They only had three rounds for the launcher, but that was more than enough to knock off a supply convoy. With luck, they would score some more.

"Here they come, buddy," he called to Kinski.

The trucks rumbled down the road in front of them. The lead truck trailed a cloud of blue smoke that clearly irritated the drivers of the two trailing trucks. Distracted by their leader's chemical assault, they didn't notice the two figures on the hillside.

Chan started the festivities. Centering the lead truck in the Christmas tree sight, Chan pulled the trigger. The long rocket blasted from the tube, the rocket motor igniting half a second later. Chan was reaching for his second rocket as the first hit the truck's cab. Hot steel fragments ripped through the cab and into the gas tank. The truck erupted in a ball of black-fringed orange flame.

Kinski's M16 was rattling. On the third truck, paint chips were flying as Kinski riddled the driver's door. He walked the burst back over the canvas cover, then dropped his weapon, picked up the AK at his feet and walked another long burst down the side of the second truck.

Chan had reloaded the RPG and fired the round into the front grille of the third truck, stopping it and trapping the second truck in the middle.

A handful of stunned FSE troops stumbled from the two riddled trucks. Short bursts from Kinski's AK sent them sprawling in the dirt.

In less than a minute, the road was quiet again, except for the crackling fire that engulfed the lead truck.

Chan and Kinski moved cautiously down to the kill zone and checked the bodies for signs of life. There were none.

The second and third trucks were full of supplies. There were crates of food, some worn furniture, mops, brooms, several cases of soap and half a truckload of mattresses.

"Fuck me running!" Kinski cursed as they surveyed the loot. "There isn't even a BB gun in here anywhere." He hooked a thumb at the bodies that littered the road. "These guys don't even have any weapons." He shook his head in disgust.

Chan sat up in the bed of the second truck and swung his feet back and forth in irritation. "This is not getting us closer to those missiles," he said, explaining the obvious.

"Well, come on," Kinski said, irritably, "let's see if there is anything at we can use in this stuff." He and Chan climbed into the truck and began to move the cleaning stuff to search the other boxes.

"Need a hand with that stuff, Buddha?" a voice asked from behind the truck.

"Sure, Jack," Chan answered, hefting a box of soap powder. Chan stopped, dropped the box and whirled. "Jack!" he hollered. Kinski was staring openmouthed at the group standing outside the truck. He and Chan jumped out of the truck, almost knocking Keenan and Mamudi down.

"We thought you were dead!" Chan shouted. "Where'd you come from?"

"We ran into some friends," Keenan answered, pointing at the two men who stood just off the road, watching for any uninvited visitors.

"The tall one is T'sinko," Mamudi introduced the men. "The other one is Kron. They're . . ."

"Spetsnaz!" Kinski blurted.

"Exactly!" Keenan said, "They saved our hash. They've been fighting the FSE for years around here."

"That's good enough for me!" Chan said stepping up to shake hands with both men.

"Me too," Kinski agreed.

"Come on," Keenan urged, "we have to get on with it. We have some new gear, thanks to these guys. Let's go!"

The six commandos quickly disappeared into the forest, leaving the three trucks burning in the road.

"Look at this stuff!" Chan crowed. He and Kinski were wandering around like pair of kids in a candy store, fingering each new toy.

"This place is the WAL-MART from Hell," Kinski observed, looking through the sights of an experimental laser rifle.

"Much of this does not work," Kron reminded them. "It was experimental equipment. Not all of it was fully developed. Still, it is better than anything the FSE is using."

"Before you get too carried away," Mamudi suggested, "we need to get back to finding those missiles." He had exchanged eyeballs today, sporting a black orb with a tiny United States flag on it. The two Russians had been quite startled by the glass eye. Mamudi had not mentioned his impairment to them.

As T'sinko spread the map over the long table, the others crowded around.

"Here is the Schloss Adler," T'sinko began. The map showed a broad, flat valley from which rose a tall, steep mountain whose flat crest was over two thousand feet higher than the valley floor. At the base of the mountain was a narrow river that ran the length of the valley.

"The fortress has many advantages," T'sinko went on, "not the least of which is the view. From its walls, any movement in the valley can be easily seen." Kron produced a large envelope of photographs and spread them on the table. "Maximov has a major force assembled, much of it around the base of the mountain," T'sinko continued. "In the fortress itself, he has a huge communication complex that relays communications throughout Europe. In addition, he also has a radar setup that covers hundreds of miles around the valley. Although there are few troops in the fortress itself, it serves as the command center for the troops stationed around it."

"How many troops are in the fort itself?" Keenan asked, picking up a photo of the tall peak. He studied it as Kron answered.

"There are only two companies of actual soldiers there," Kron explained. "They guard the cable car terminal and the small antiaircraft unit."

Keenan passed the photo to Mamudi. "Why does this place look so familiar?" he asked. Mamudi shook his head. Kinski reached for the photo and answered.

"I know what it looks like to me," he said. "It looks just like the mountain in that movie *Close Encounters*."

Keenan nodded. The forbidding mountain looked just like the Devil's Tower in America, even down to the fluted sides and flaring rubble pile at its base.

"Jack," Buddha Chan asked, "how the hell are we going to get up there? They sure aren't going to sell us a ticket on the cable car."

"We could climb it," Keenan answered. "It's steep, but I knew a guy once who climbed the cliff up to Ft. Ticonderoga on an exercise. It was steep, too, but they managed to do it at night and surprised the hell out the guys on top."

"I'll bet that cliff wasn't ringed with troops looking for his ass, either," Chan observed. Keenan nodded ruefully in agreement.

"Perhaps a cheap trick could gain us access to the cable car?" Mamudi suggested. "We could dress in FSE uniforms and commandeer the car."

"Right," Kinski said, caught up in the idea. "One or two of us could get in there and then bring up the rest!"

"I still think it would be easier to climb it!" Keenan insisted.

The argument continued long into the night.

"How long until they are ready?" Maximov asked as he did every morning.

Ivan Virograd, Maximov's missile expert, shook his head and gave the same answer he always did. "Not until I can duplicate the computer linkage I need to program and fire them. There is no way to predict how long that will take."

"Days?" Maximov snapped. "Weeks? Months? What?"

"Days," Virograd answered, "perhaps weeks."

Maximov fumed, looking out the tall, narrow window at the two canvas-covered missiles. Now that he actually had them in his grasp, he urgently wanted to use them, or at least one of them.

He would blast London with one and kill Shatterhand. That would cripple the allied resistance to him. With London in flames, no one would dare oppose him. That thought sent sexual shivers through Maximov's body. He turned to the scientist.

"Days, Virograd," he barked. "I want them in days, not weeks!"

"Yes, Chairman Maximov," the scientist replied meekly. "I will not fail you."

"See that you do not," Maximov warned as he left the man to his computers.

• • •

The wind had shifted to the north, plunging the temperatures to near freezing.

"Winter always come on so soon?" Keenan asked as he and T'sinko watched the clouds race by overhead.

"No," the Russian answered, "not for another month, at least."

"Great!" Keenan smiled. "It'll keep those troops around the mountain close to their fires!"

T'sinko smiled. "You think like a Spetsnaz, Keenan," he observed. "Bad weather is good weather to attack in, eh?"

"You bet!" Keenan answered. "Let's get cracking." They set off for the small town of Gherm, six kilometers away. In Gherm there was an alehouse and house of ill repute favored by FSE officers and political flunkies. They would find the uniforms they needed there.

FIFTEEN

Irma Kringle grimaced as she wiped her mouth with the back of her hand. "Pig!" she muttered under her breath as she refilled the four large steins with foaming beer. She shook her head, wondering how the girls upstairs could bring themselves to sleep with such awful creatures. Even whores should have better taste. Just having one kiss her made Irma want to puke.

As she brought the beer back to the table, the men were singing some nasty song about virgins. She ignored them and dodged their roving hands as she put the beer on the table. As she spun out of their grasp, one of them, a huge man who spoke German with a Russian accent, stood and raised his beer stein.

"Come my friends," he shouted. "Drink up!" He jerked his head in Irma's direction. "If our little friend here does not want to play, I know where there are others who will!"

The others hooted in agreement and drained their beers, spilling much of it on their tunics in the process. Irma smiled. The whores could deal with them now, and she would get a rest.

Besides, they were lousy tippers. A handful of coins was all she had to show for hauling beer for them all afternoon and she had had to fish them out of the top of her dress where they had dropped them. Good riddance!

As she cleared away the empty steins from the table, she looked out the window at the setting sun. The feeble light

92 *Michael McGann*

glanced through thick clouds on the horizon, giving the small town a plain, one-color look that made its broken streets and dilapidated buildings seem even more pathetic than they really were.

I need to get out of here, Irma thought, but to where?

Keenan stamped his feet to keep the blood flowing. He and T'sinko had been standing in the shadows next to the deserted mill since sunset. The wind was beginning to cut through his BDUs and field jacket. His hypersensitive skin felt the cold even more and he could not seem to ignore the sensation.

"I hope these ol' boys don't party all night!" he hissed. He could see T'sinko grin in the darkness.

"I doubt that they have that much stamina!" he chuckled softly, "They do not seem . . ."

He stopped in mid-sentence. They watched through the alehouse windows as four men staggered downstairs and made their way toward the door, singing loudly.

Keenan and T'sinko silently readied their weapons and slipped deeper into the shadows to wait for the men to come back to their car, parked in front of the mill a few meters away.

T'sinko carried his own silenced Makarov 9mm pistol. Keenan had picked up one of the weapons in the lab. It was built on a shotgun frame, but fired a rimmed, hand-loaded version of the .45 Long Colt cartridge. The barrel was surrounded by a silencer tube that ran the length of the 12 inch barrel and another half a foot beyond. A black plastic foregrip worked the short slide action.

The weapon made no sound when it fired, only the soft clicking of the slide action as an empty shell was ejected and a live one fed into the chamber. The short magazine held five shots.

The four men rolled out the door of the alehouse and weaved toward the parked Audi. When they were halfway to the car, the alehouse door opened and a woman came out.

The four men looked around and called to her but she ignored them. Keenan looked at his Soviet companion. T'sinko was smiling like a wolf, watching his prey as they came closer. Keenan also noticed that he wasn't cold any more.

• • •

Finally, the pigs were leaving and she could go home, too. As the drunks paid old Hoffer, the alehouse owner, Irma went to the kitchen, pulled off her apron and reached for her coat.

They were gone when she came back and she waved to Hoffer as she made for the door. Outside, the cold hit her and she pulled her thin coat tighter around her. The drunks were weaving across the street toward a nice four-door sedan parked in front of the old mill.

"Bastards," she muttered. "You ride in nice cars while the rest of us walk in the cold." The four drunks called to her, alcoholically suggesting that she join them to continue their party. She ignored them.

An odd sound made her turn back. One of the drunks was lying on the ground.

Passed out, she thought. Just then, another of the drunks pitched backward, then another. The big man, the one who had kissed her, looked at his comrades then at the dark shadows next to the mill.

Irma saw one shadow detach itself from the others. There was a faint clicking sound. The big man's head exploded, the grisly contents spraying out behind him. He fell backward, contents of his skull filling a muddy pothole in the road.

From the shadows, two men stepped around the car and knelt quickly beside each fallen drunk. They felt quickly for any sign of life, then rifled through the dead men's pockets until they found the key to the car.

The two men gathered up the bodies and piled them into the car, two in the backseat and two in the trunk. This done, the strangers climbed into the front seat and started the car.

Irma stood rooted to the spot by fear. She hadn't actually seen anyone die since the war and she had never seen anyone killed so simply before at all. There had been no shots and the dead men hadn't made a sound, either.

As she stood in the road with her mouth open and her eyes wide with fear, the sedan pulled alongside her.

A big man with red hair leaned out and smiled at her.

"Sorry to upset you," he said happily in English. "Can we give you a lift somewhere?"

She shook her head no. The big man smiled and waved at her as he drove away. She stood watching the car's taillights until they turned off and disappeared. Irma realized her mouth was still open, the cold air drying her throat. She gulped, swallowed and ran for home.

Now you have to get out of here, she thought as she ran.

They had been lucky. The big man's uniform fit Keenan just fine and one of the others had been Kinski's size. The blood and mud had come out of the fabric easily and now the uniforms were ready for their new owners.

"How do I look?" Kinski asked, striking a Vogue model pose in his FSE suit.

"Like an Elvis impersonator in a FSE drag show," Chan observed caustically. Kinski frowned.

"You're just jealous because there weren't any chubby dwarfs in that bunch so you could have a new outfit too," Kinski countered, pulling his comb and running it through his hair's frontal wave.

"I'm sure that's it!" Chan answered, sobbing unrealistically.

"Knock it off, guys," Keenan ordered. "We need to get cracking on this if we're going to get it to work!"

On the long table, Kron and T'sinko were putting the finishing touches on a pencil drawing of the cable car terminal on the ground and the cable house at the castle.

"Okay," Keenan said. "Let's run through it again with the drawing."

Kinski stepped up to the table. "You, me and Kron bluff our way through here," he said, pointing to the terminal building, "then you and I go up to the castle and knock out the crew there."

"Once you get up there"—Chan took up the story—"me and Mamudi come up in the second car to help with the heavy artillery."

"And leave the terminal to us," Kron jumped in.

"When we are all together in the castle," Mamudi went on, "we knock out the missiles, wreck what we can in the castle, leave a time charge in the cable house and come back down in the car."

"After which, we blow up the cable car terminal," T'sinko completed the plan.

"Right," Keenan smiled. "Simple, huh?"

The others gave him a look that suggested that they were skeptical.

SIXTEEN

Vlad Kilnikov was freezing. The small stove in the terminal glowed weakly, but put out very little heat. There had been no activity in the terminal since that morning, when another group of FSE dignitaries had gone up to see the chairman's new prizes.

Now, as the sun dropped low on the horizon, the temperature outside was falling rapidly and Kilnikov was chilled to the bone.

At least I'm inside, he admitted. The two guards outside had their collars up and their hat flaps down to fight off the biting wind that swept down from the north.

Outside, a car pulled up and parked next to the terminal. Two officers got out and pulled a prisoner out of the backseat. They saluted their way past the sentries outside, pushing the prisoner ahead of them.

As the two officers walked up to him, Kilnikov snapped to attention. The shorter man, a major, returned the salute, then coughed, doubling over as he brought his hand up to his face. Kilnikov stepped forward as the major straightened up.

"Herr Major?" he asked. The prisoner, who was dressed in some strange foreign uniform, his fingers laced behind his head, laughed.

"You better call the car down before this pig catches pneumonia!" the captive shouted in Russian.

"Shut up!" the tall, red-haired officer snapped. He stepped forward and slapped the prisoner across the head. The man laughed again.

"At once!" Kilnikov answered, smiling. Ordinarily, he would have asked for identification and orders, but there were so many VIPs going up lately and they were so surly when questioned that Kilnikov had stopped asking questions at all.

He pressed the intercom switch and called up to the castle to send down the car. A moment later, the big wheel above them began to turn as the cable brought down the car.

Kilnikov never saw the pistol in the coughing officer's hand, never heard the quiet cough it made as it popped a half-inch hole just over his right temple. He fell like a tree, dropping out of sight behind the counter.

Chan and Mamudi walked slowly down the deserted street that sloped gently toward the terminal building. They didn't want to get there too early while the guards were still outside.

Through the wide side window of the building, they saw Kinski kill the guard inside. They picked up the pace as Kinski turned and walked to the front doors.

They were even with the two outside guards as Kinski opened the door and spoke to the guard on the right. The man turned just in time to see Kinski's silenced pistol come up and fire. The fur hat, its ear flaps tied securely under his chin, kept the hapless guard's head from coming apart when the heavy bullet blew through his left eye into his brain.

The other guard, stunned by the silent death of his comrade, reached for the rifle slung on his shoulder. His eyes widened as Mamudi's blade slid through the heavy topcoat and up into his heart. Mamudi held the man close as he twisted the knife back and forth, cutting the bottom out of the guard's ventricles.

The man's eyes rolled back and Mamudi caught his weight. Chan was already pushing the other guard's dead body into the terminal. In moments, both dead guards were inside. Kinski walked out and opened the car trunk. T'sinko slipped out and helped Kinski pull a large nylon bag from the trunk. They carried the bag between them back inside.

The terminal was taken. So far, so good.

Inside, Keenan was watching as the car descended from the castle. It took several minutes to make the trip down.

"As long as they don't want to talk to anybody, we're okay," Keenan said hopefully. Behind them, the two Spetsnaz had already taken up positions at the door.

The egg-shaped car clattered into the terminal and slowly stopped at the platform. Keenan pulled the door open and held it as Kinski and Mamudi wrestled the heavy bag into the cable car.

"I still think we all ought to go up at once," Chan urged. "If you get into deep *kemchi* up there, we won't be able to help you."

"We'll be okay," Keenan answered. "Just be ready when the other car comes down."

"We will be ready, Jack," Mamudi assured him. Keenan slid the door shut and pressed the red button in the car. The big wheel overhead began to rotate again and the tiny car started back up to the Schloss Adler high above.

Rolf Steiner watched through his binoculars as the car started back up from the terminal. Inside, two men lounged against the windows, looking, as all passengers did, at the amazing view from the cable car.

"Where is the other man?" he asked himself. He had seen three men get out of the car earlier. One had his hands behind his head, as if he was a prisoner. Now there were only two. He watched as the car ascended up the steel cable. Curious.

Steiner turned to the soldier who stood at the power console.

"Call down to the terminal," he ordered. "Ask Kilnikov how many other passengers are waiting."

The soldier stepped over to the intercom and pressed the talk switch, repeating Steiner's message. After a moment, he pressed the switch and repeated it again.

"What did he say?" Chan asked nervously.

"He is asking the agent," Kron answered, gesturing with his thumb at the dead man behind the counter, "how many other passengers we have here."

"Uh oh," Chan observed.

"Indeed," T'sinko agreed as he stepped over to the intercom

and answered. He spoke in Russian, trying to pass for the dead
FSE soldier lying behind the counter.

"Captain Steiner," the soldier at the intercom called, "they
say there are no more passengers in the terminal." The soldier
stepped forward and leaned over the rail. "It did not sound like
Kilnikov on the other end, Captain," he said.

Steiner watched the car. It was halfway up to the castle now.
There had been plenty of unusual visitors lately, but he had a
feeling about these two.

"Stop the car!" Steiner barked. The wheelman pulled the
throttle lever toward him, cutting the power to the huge electric
motors that turned the cable drum.

Steiner stepped up to the intercom panel and switched it to
speak to the passengers in the car.

"This is Captain Rolf Steiner in the Schloss Adler," he introduced himself. "Please identify yourself and state the nature of
your visit to FSE headquarters!"

"Looks like we're stuck," Keenan moaned, "I'm open to
suggestions."

"I don't think we got a choice," Kinski answered, kneeling
to unzip the large bag. "We need to un-ass this car!" Kinski
pulled a square parcel from the bag and twisted a clock face
on the front of it.

Keenan was pulling the nylon web belt off his uniform. "I
guess we get to take the cable down," he observed. "It's way
too far to jump!"

"Roger that," Kinski agreed, standing and pulling at his
belt.

Steiner watched the activity in the car. The men had not
answered, but seemed to be quite busy. Steiner called to the
guards outside the terminal door. The two soldiers ran to the
rail where Steiner stood watching.

"Fire a shot into the car!" Steiner instructed the men. Both
soldiers put their AKs to their shoulders and fired. The glass
shattered in two of the car's windows.

"That's our cue to exit," Keenan shouted as the glass splattered around the inside of the car. "The next ones will get us!"

"I'm right ahead of you," Kinski quipped as he pulled down the window that faced the terminal from which they had just come. He flipped the web belt over the greasy cable and caught the free end. Using the belt for support, he pulled his feet up and swung out the window.

"YAAAHHHHAAA!" he yelled as he slid away down the cable. The wound in his arm stretched and popped open again. He could feel the warm blood running down the inside of his sleeve toward his armpit. There was some pain, but it took a backseat to the rush of sliding down half a mile of steel cable a thousand feet up.

Keenan followed a moment later. The two men dropped away from the car, the steep angle of the steel cable presenting little friction as they slid along it.

"I was afraid of something like this!" Mamudi hissed as the car stopped in midair. He watched as the car dangled in space, swaying gently back and forth on the thick cable. Next to him, Chan slipped his arm through the M14's sling and adjusted the yellow shooter's glasses on his nose.

As the two Marauders watched, something seemed to jump inside the cable car. A few seconds later, the two pops echoed down from the castle above.

"That's it!" Chan barked. He stepped over to the open cable car door and braced himself against the wall, squinting through the slim telescope on his rifle. A second later, it barked as Chan opened fire on the cable car terminal high above in the castle.

Steiner watched in disbelief as the two figures dropped from the car, sliding down the cable.

"Fire on those men!" he shouted. The two riflemen took aim again. As one fired, the other spun around, a wet red gooey spot where his nose had been.

Steiner looked back at the car, staring in disbelief. He raised his binoculars as the remaining rifleman fired at the two figures, who now were picking up speed as they hurtled down the slick cable. Steiner flicked the binoculars toward the ground terminal just in time to see a small orange flash.

"Fire at the terminal," Steiner blurted. The guard turned, gagged and slumped against Steiner.

The AK fell from the man's hands as Steiner tried to catch him. There was a small hole in the man's jacket just over his heart. It suddenly dawned on Steiner that he would be number three with a bullet. He flung himself to the floor as a slug screamed off the metal wall behind him.

"Bring that car up!" Steiner screamed at the motorman.

The river was coming up fast below them. Kinski was looking straight down between his feet, watching the ground rush past. As he crossed the river bank, he let go of the web belt.

"AAAHHHHAAWWW!" he again observed as he fell the last hundred feet to the icy water below. He slammed feet first into the black water. The cold water stunned him, taking his breath away. As he broke the surface a few seconds later, Keenan slammed into the water beside him like a human cannonball.

"Jack!" Kinski screamed as the red-haired giant disappeared beneath the water. Kinski thrashed around, searching for Keenan in the dark water. A rifle cracked from the cable car terminal ahead of them. Buddha Chan's M14 was covering them. Keenan popped to the surface a few feet away, gasping from the cold.

"Come on!" he shouted as the current swept them both along. "Swim!"

As they swam frantically for the far bank, Chan's rifle kept up a steady covering fire at the castle.

"Come, friends!" T'sinko shouted. "We have company!" Outside a squad of FSE soldiers were running up the street, attracted by the gunfire. The two Spetsnaz stepped through the two front doorways of the cable car terminal. Their G-11s barked, sending twin streams of tiny, hyper-velocity slugs down the street. The dozen FSE troops never knew what hit them. The needle-like bullets ripped through their heavy jackets and tore at their flesh, exploding their organs and gouging huge holes in their wakes.

T'sinko ran for the car and dove into the driver's seat as Kron covered him. As the sedan roared to life, Mamudi and Chan followed Kron as he dashed for the car. Once inside, T'sinko gunned the engine and sped down the street. Behind them, shots rang out as other FSE troops responded to the shooting. Hanging out the windows, Kron and Chan returned the fire. Several FSE dropped as the sedan roared away, headed for the river.

He could still hear the shooting below, but it was not coming at him anymore. Steiner peeked cautiously over the edge. The car was on its way up, empty. He focused his binoculars on the ground terminal. In the street in front of the terminal, a group of soldiers were firing at a sedan that was speeding away. As he watched, several of the soldiers crumpled to the ground.

Steiner turned his binoculars to the river. Downstream, the two figures were struggling toward the far bank.

"There!" Mamudi shouted, pointing to the two men struggling up the bank. T'sinko swerved off the road toward Keenan and Kinski, the car sliding in the soft dirt. The pair was trying to run, their soaked uniforms dragging at them. Mamudi was out the door before the car stopped, running for his friends.

"Come on," he urged, grabbing both men by their jackets and propelling them toward the waiting car. "We must make haste!"

Keenan growled something in return, but Mamudi could not make it out. Their dripping jackets felt like ice to the touch. They stumbled toward the waiting Audi, slipping on the soft, wet earth. Kron and Chan were outside the car, covering the road.

"Let's go!" Mamudi shouted as he pushed Keenan and Kinski into the car, one in the front seat and one in back. Kron and Chan whirled back into the car.

"Oww!" Kinski howled as the two big men nearly squashed him between them.

"Oohh!" Chan exclaimed as the icy water from Kinski's clothes soaked through his own. "Jesus, that's cold!"

"Y-you ought to be in h-here with it!" Kinski wailed, his teeth chattering as his body shook from the cold. Kron took Kinski's hand and began to rub it vigorously between his own to restore the circulation. On the other side, Chan did the same.

"Th-thanks, guys," Kinski stammered.

• • •

In the terminal, Steiner was again on the intercom to the ground terminal.

"Three dead here, Captain," the guard sergeant reported, "and nearly a dozen killed outside."

"Secure the terminal!" Steiner ordered, "and this time, really secure it! Do you understand me, Sergeant?"

"Exactly so!" the sergeant answered. "It is done!"

Steiner hung up the phone as the riddled cable car slowly entered the terminal. After the two intruders had escaped, Steiner brought the car up to search it for anything that might identify the two men.

As the car stopped, Pvt. Bekker stepped over to the door, reaching for the handle.

"Stop!" Steiner screamed, stepping behind the operating console, "You fool! That door might be booby-trapped! Look inside first!"

Bekker made a complete circuit of the car, inspecting the door from the windows.

"There is nothing on the door, Herr Captain," he reported, "or the handle."

"Open it!" Steiner barked, ducking slightly behind the console just in case.

Bekker pulled open the door, cringing visibly as he did so. Inside, the car was empty.

"Is there anything in it?" Steiner asked from behind the console.

Bekker shot a look toward the console, a look that said, "chickenshit officers." He looked around inside the car. Under the seat at the far end was a big blue nylon bag. "There is a bag in here, Herr Captain," Bekker answered. "Should I check it?"

"Yes," Steiner answered from behind the console. "Get in the car and wait for my order. Do not touch the bag until I say to!"

Bekker looked like a Thanksgiving Day turkey in an FSE suit for a second, then shrugged and stepped into the car and sat down on the bench seat across the car from the blue bag.

Steiner looked over at the cable operator. "Send the car outside the terminal fifty meters!" he ordered. The cable operator pushed the big lever forward, engaging the wheel that moved the cable. The car shuddered and started back out of the station. A few moments later, it stopped, swinging gently back and forth on the heavy cable.

Steiner stood and stepped back over the intercom panel.

"Bekker!" he barked. "Open the bag cautiously! Check it for traps!"

Muttering a very graphic description of Steiner's mother, Bekker slowly unzipped the nylon bag a few inches, then slid his hand into the bag, gently feeling for any wires or pressure devices waiting inside. There were none.

He unzipped the bag. Inside were half a dozen LAW's rockets and a few square satchel charges. Two strange green plastic rifles and a pair of web belt suspenders were the only other items. Bekker stepped back to the intercom by the door.

"There are no traps, Herr Captain," he said, trying to keep the reproach out of his voice, "only rifles, rocket launchers and some explosive charges."

"Well done, Bekker!" Steiner's voice crackled over the speaker. Bekker heard him tell the operator to bring the car back in. He sat on the bench above the seat as the car rocked back to life. Bekker reached into the bag and took out one of the strange rifles. He looked at it for a second, then laid it on the seat and took out a satchel charge. The charge was in a canvas bag with a carrying strap. There was no fuse lighter visible.

As the car entered the terminal, Bekker unsnapped the flap that covered the top and front of the bag. On top of the charge, a timer block sat nestled in the thick slabs of plastic explosive. The timer glowed red. Bekker turned it up to look at it. The red numbers 003 glowed on the timer's face. As the numbers turned to 002, Bekker screamed, dropped the charge and dashed for the door.

"BOMB!" he screamed as he wrenched at the handle. His scream was lost in the blast that followed. Thirty pounds of plastic explosive detonated in the bag, setting off the rockets stored below.

Bekker vanished as the car erupted into thousands of metal bits that flew from the black high-explosive cloud. The explosion shattered the terminal and shredded Steiner, the operator and the remaining guards.

The heat of the explosion burned through the cable above the car. The heavy cable dropped from the terminal and fell in a long, graceful arc down to the valley floor below. Pieces of the ruined terminal followed the cable, decorating the lower slope of the mountain with twisted debris.

T'sinko blasted through the town unchallenged by other FSE. Behind them, a boom echoed across the valley. Kron, Kinski and Chan strained to turn their heads, looking back toward the sound. Smoke was pouring from the castle's cable car terminal. The long black cable was nearly to the valley floor, falling like a thin black scythe.

"Y-YEAH!" Kinski shouted. "We knocked out the terminal, Jack!" He reached up to slap Keenan's wet shoulder. Keenan, trapped between T'sinko and Mamudi, nodded.

"They will not take anything up to the Schloss Adler that way," Kron observed as flames licked out of the smoking cable house. "At least . . ."

"We didn't get the missiles," Keenan interrupted. "That's all that really matters." He tried to turn his head to look back at the others. "We still gotta do that!"

The others in the car were silent. Kinski broke the silence. "And we just blew up the only way to get up there."

SEVENTEEN

"The terminal is heavily damaged, Chairman Maximov," Colonel Carl Probst, the commander of Schloss Adler, explained. "The winding mechanism is still intact, although we do not know yet if it can be made operational again. The controls are ruined. They will have to be replaced."

Maximov sat with his hands pressed together, the fingers pointed upward, almost like a man at prayer. He sat silently listening to the litany of loss.

"We lost nearly two dozen dead," Probst went on, "including Captain Steiner, the cable car terminal staff, and those killed in the attack on the ground terminal."

"I am not concerned about the cable car staff or the damage estimates, Colonel," Maximov snapped. "I want to know when the damage will be repaired!" He stood and looked out Probst's office window at the valley spread out below them. "We are trapped here like rats until then!"

"True, Comrade Chairman," Probst said placatingly, "but well-fed, comfortable rats who are well protected from any further attack."

"What do you have to do to repair the cable?" Maximov asked, turning from the window to fix Probst with a glare as icy as the wind that howled outside.

"If the winding mechanism can be repaired," Probst explained, "we can pull the cable back up and re-attach it. We would then have one operable car until we could find another to replace the one that was destroyed. Bringing up the cable would take a week, perhaps ten days."

"I want it fixed by the end of the week," Maximov snarled as he strode toward the carved oak door. "You have four days to repair the cable." He stopped at the door. "Or you will take the same trip it did!"

"Yes, Comrade Chairman," Probst answered as the heavy door slammed shut. Probst sat quietly for a moment, then stepped to the window and opened it, letting in the cold blast from outside. The oppressive heaviness that had come with Maximov's visit slowly dissipated in the freezing air.

"W-well," Keenan chattered, "s-so much for that great idea!" The big man sat huddled over a small electric heater.

Kinski sat across from him, his hands held close to the heater's glowing wires. Mamudi had bandaged Kinski's re-opened wound, tying the flesh-colored field dressing in place. Now, a tiny rivulet of blood cautiously sneaked down his bicep.

In the lab's kitchen, Kron and Mamudi were opening ration boxes, converting the experimental grub into real food. "Bad luck, I would say," Kron observed. "The plan was sound."

"You still achieved more than you think," T'sinko, sitting nearby smoking a cigarette, speculated. "You have bottled up the missiles, their technical staff and their high command in one place. You are now in a position to inflict serious damage upon the FSE."

Keenan snorted. "The only position I can see us in is bent over, holding our ankles!"

T'sinko laughed, blowing smoke through his nose. "Well, my friend, one battle does not make a campaign and one butt-fucking does not make a love affair!" Everyone laughed at that, even Keenan.

"Come on, you philosophers," Mamudi called from the kitchen, "soup's on!" The hot food had a warming effect both on Keenan's frozen body and his flagging spirits. An hour later, he was brainstorming with Chan and the two Russians, searching for another plan.

"I don't see any way to do this without climbing that mountain and hauling up enough firepower to knock out those missiles!" Chan complained.

"I doubt that the FSE will allow you to do that," Kron argued, "now that they know that you are here. They will surely step up their security on the mountain for just that reason."

"I think it might work just because it *is* so unlikely!" Keenan interjected. "They won't think anyone is so stupid to try it!"

"I do not think I would like to bet on the reasoning powers of the FSE," Kron said.

"Nor I," Mamudi agreed. "They have a virtual lock on stupid maneuvers, Jack. If they didn't, we wouldn't be alive!"

Keenan smiled. That was true. The Marauders were good, but it helped that the FSE was so bad.

"I believe that this discussion has been made superfluous," T'sinko commented. He was standing next to a small weather data panel near the door. "The barometer is falling, and so is the temperature outside. I believe we may be in for some bad weather."

"Why don't we get some sleep and try again in the morning?" Mamudi suggested. There were no arguments.

The next morning confirmed T'sinko's suspicions. Outside, a light rain was turning to sleet, coating the hills and forest with a sheen of ice.

Inside, the talk now was of alternate plans to try to exploit the ice storm and gain access to the castle.

Finally warm again, but bored with all the tactical masturbation, Kinski set out to explore the lab's many storerooms, looking for more exotic equipment.

Two of the storerooms were filled with an assortment of tents and sleeping bags, many of them damaged from the testing process. There were boxes of boots and thermal underwear, odd-looking ponchos that turned into bivi-sacks and other useful, but boring, paraphernalia. Kinski, only recently thawed out, took a set of insulated underwear.

The third storeroom looked like a replay of the first two. There were lightweight rucksacks and fancy body armor vests and some long, thin nylon bags that Kinski almost ignored. He unzipped the nearest bag and looked inside at the strange collection of carbon fiber poles and heavy nylon fabric. It took him a minute to find the data panel sewn on the dark cloth.

"HO-LY SHIT!" Kinski hollered.

The five men turned their heads toward the hallway as Kinski dashed around the corner, beaming.

"Pete!" Keenan scolded. "If you're not going to help think of something, at least don't interrupt the rest of us, okay?"

"Come here, boss man," Kinski smiled. "I got the answer to our problem!"

They helped Kinski drag the long nylon bags and a pair of large square bags out into the open bay. He opened one and pulled out the poles and nylon, then set about constructing the strange device. In two minutes, Kinski had a large, bat-winged glider assembled. Its wingtips nearly filled the bay.

"What the hell is it?" Chan asked.

"Hang glider!" Kinski answered. "It's like the ones we used to use back home, but bigger." Kinski unzipped one of the square bags. "This gismo is an engine that fits on the glider and turns it into a little bitty airplane!"

"Very pretty," Chan observed. "But what's the point?"

"Don't be a linear thinker, Buddha," Kinski chided. "We can use these things to get into the castle! We can literally drop in on 'em!"

"Oh, right," Chan argued, "like this little piss-ant glider could take us all up there with our gear and the FSE wouldn't even notice!" He gave Kinski a look of extreme annoyance.

"I thought you had to have a mountain to launch hang gliders from in the first place," Mamudi said.

"Not these guys!" Kinski answered. "The motors get them up to altitude, then you cut of the motor and glide!" He walked over to the other bags. "There's four gliders here and two motor kits. We can tow the two unpowered ones behind the powered ones!"

"This is a pretty far-out idea, Pete," Keenan observed.

"Not really," T'sinko commented. "The Germans used gliders to attack a Belgian fortress at the beginning of the Great Patriotic War, what you call World War Two." As all eyes turned to him, T'sinko went on. "The Germans landed their gliders on the flat roof of the fortress and fought their way down inside from the top. The defenders were completely surprised and the fortress, which was a huge, formidable place, was taken. It was a brilliant tactical move."

"How is it that you always seem to know so much, T'sinko?" Chan asked. "You're just filled with information."

T'sinko smiled. "It is because the Spetsnaz studied military organizations other than our own, and battles in which we did not participate!" Chan still looked confused, but Keenan chuckled knowingly.

"So whadda ya think?" Kinski asked anxiously.

"In lieu of any better plan," Keenan answered, "I think we need to see if this'll work." Kinski beamed and ran his metal comb through his damaged, but stylish coiffure.

Yevgeny Maximov looked at the clouds that swirled around the Schloss Adler and smiled, then frowned. Behind him, Carl Probst sat nervously waiting for the chairman to speak.

"This weather is a two-edged sword, eh, Probst?" Maximov asked rhetorically.

"How so, Comrade Chairman?" Probst answered tentatively.

"It slows the repair of the cable car, but it also keeps our attackers at bay."

"Indeed, Comrade Chairman," Probst agreed.

Maximov turned from the window. "You know that our new weapons will be ready to launch within the next two days!" Probst nodded. Maximov smiled, looking beyond Probst at a distant but pleasant vision.

"After that, the rebels and the pathetic English king will have no choice!" Maximov proclaimed. "They will kneel before the FSE, or they will perish in nuclear fire!"

The Chairman's eyes were glowing, his mouth working, a faint sheen of sweat on his face even in the cold office. Probst suddenly remembered his father's description of the man he had served in another war. That man sought total domination, too. Probst's father had described the man's eyes, the intense stare and barely controlled inner rage. Now, like his father before him, Probst was in the presence of a madman who sought to dominate the world.

What is it about us, Probst asked himself, that makes us love these bullies?

"I don't know, Pete," Chan said nervously. "This thing doesn't look like it can really fly."

"It'll fly, Buddha," Kinski replied. "You just watch!" Kinski had strapped on the thin harness and now held the glider up with one hand as he clipped himself to its frame.

"What kind of engine is this?" Mamudi asked as he ran his hand down the short graphite propellor. The engine, mounted on a fiberglass tripod atop the glider, was about the size of a soccer ball.

"It's a chainsaw engine!" Kinski answered. "Only it has a mega-muffler on it to keep the noise down." Kinski spread his feet and got a firm grip on the control yoke.

"Okay, start me up!" he said, flipping the engine switch. Keenan stepped over to the tiny engine. He pulled the starter cord once, then again. The tiny engine sputtered to life and Kinski worked the hand throttle to keep it running.

"Here goes nothing!" Kinski called above the engine whine. He hefted the glider up, gunned the little engine and took a few running steps forward. To everyone's amazement, the glider lifted him off the ground and soared slowly, almost majestically, into the night sky. In a minute, Kinski had disappeared into the darkness above them.

"Un-fuckin'-believable!" Chan muttered. In a moment, the sound of the small engine was lost in the murmuring of the wind. Keenan searched the dark sky, looking with his heightened senses for the glider. Finally he found it, directly overhead. Kinski had turned off the engine. The others were oblivious to him slipping through the air a hundred feet above them. Keenan watched as Kinski turned the glider and circled slowly around, coming up behind them. At the last second, Kinski flared the glider and literally dropped out of the sky as gently as stepping out of bed.

"TA-DA!" Kinski sang out, catching the weight of the glider as it settled to the ground. The group whirled around, surprised by his silent appearance.

Kinski unclipped his harness and stepped out from under the glider. "Death from Above!" he cheered.

"Hair-do from Hell!" Chan retorted.

"Whatever," Kinski replied, taking a modest bow. "Now help me take this thing apart before we attract any attention." In minutes, the glider was back in its carry bag and the six men were back in the lab.

Rupert Morgenau was asleep in his chair when the radar warning tone warbled. As his head snapped up, his eyes snapped open, furiously studying his screen as he forced the rest of his body awake. He had heard the tone, although it had been weak, almost uncertain. Where was the aircraft? There was no discrete blip on the green phosphor screen, only a hazy patch of faint yellow light on the bottom of the scope. That spot lit up from time to time due to ground clutter.

"What?" Klaus Templar, the air defense coordinator called down on the intercom. Templar had a warning tone speaker in his quarters to wake him if an intruder showed up on the radar.

"I do not know, mein Herr," Morgenau replied, hoping the sleep was gone from his voice. "There was a faint tone, but there is no target on the screen."

"Increase the distance scan," Templar ordered.

"Increasing," Morgenau replied, switching the radar to its farthest scanning range. Again only the hazy patch of ground clutter lit the screen. "Nothing," Morgenau reported again.

For a moment, Templar was silent. "What do you have on the screen?" he asked.

"Only the usual ground clutter, Herr Templar," Morgenau answered. His body was vibrating now from the sudden rush of adrenaline into his sleeping system.

"It's probably the weather," Templar said after another short silence. "Ice can do that sometimes. Keep a sharp watch on it and report any changes to me."

"*Ja wohl, mein Herr*," Morgenau answered. He would have no trouble staying awake now.

"They'll pick us up on radar as soon as we clear the trees!" Chan protested.

"Not really," Keenan answered. He held up one of the glider's wing spars. "This baby's made of synthetics throughout. They don't show up on radar very well."

"What about the engine and propellor?" Mamudi asked. "The engine is metal."

"Aluminum," Kinski answered. "The prop's epoxy-bound graphite. It's a stealth hang glider!"

"Hang this!" Chan suggested. He grabbed himself between the legs.

"Okay, assuming these things fly, and radar won't pick 'em up, will they carry anything besides us?" Keenan asked.

"The non-powered ones are rated for 300 pounds," Kinski explained. "The powered ones for 400 pounds. They'll carry us and enough goodies to do the job."

"What sort of goodies?" Chan asked.

"We have a smorgasbord from which to choose," Mamudi interrupted. "This lab is full of destructive devices. Assuming our hosts will permit us to partake of them."

The four Americans looked at the two Russians who stood a few feet away, silently listening to the conversation.

"Feel free to use whatever you need," T'sinko offered. "After all, they did belong to your country once!"

"Indeed," Keenan replied. He looked back at the others. "T'sinko, you and I will figure out what we're going to need to take out the missiles. Kinski will figure out how to get us there—and back. And," he grimaced, "it would help if we knew anything about the layout of that fort."

"It is deeply reassuring that you are concerned with coming back," Mamudi offered.

"Yeah," Kinski agreed, "since it's the only way we'll ever get laid again!" On that note, they broke up into groups and went about their separate tasks.

EIGHTEEN

The idea woke Kinski up at 3:00 A.M. They needed a recon of the fortress, but there was no way to get a look inside it. Or was there? The idea was simple. He'd do a photo fly-by over the fortress on the glider! Kinski slipped out of his cot and quietly walked down to the optical lab. T'sinko had shown them a small 35mm infrared camera there. The camera was still on the padded bench, a handful of film rolls next to it. Kinski pocketed the film and hung the camera around his neck.

As quietly as he could, he took the bags containing the glider and the motor assembly and stacked them by the door. This done, he slipped on the insulated underwear, pulled on a pair of dark coveralls, and slipped quietly out the door.

Back inside the lab, Jack Keenan woke suddenly, wondering if he had actually heard the door to the lab open or not. He knew the door was sealed from inside. The two Russians were very compulsive about that. He lay listening for more sounds for a moment. The lab was silent except for Chan's snores. Keenan was about to roll over and forget about it when he thought of Kinski. An odd feeling swept over him, a premonition or something.

Probably just nerves, he told himself. You're worried about finding a plan to get into that fort. Just ignore this and get some sleep so you can think tomorrow. He rolled over and tried to put the feeling out of his mind. It didn't work. Keenan suddenly sat bolt upright, jumped off his cot and ran to the next room. Kinski's bunk was empty. The feeling was not just nerves!

Keenan stepped back into the hall and shouted, "Kinski!" The only reply was a flurry of moans and the scuffling of feet. The two Russians burst from their room, rifles in hand. Behind him, Keenan heard the click-clack of Chan's rifle bolt.

"What's up, Jack?" Mamudi's voice asked from the darkness behind him.

"Kinski's gone!" Keenan said. "I had this weird feeling."

"Gone where?" T'sinko asked, concern and a bit of mistrust in his voice.

Keenan heard the change in tone and looked at the Soviet officer. "Don't worry about Kinski going over to the other side," Keenan reassured the tall Russian. "He's no traitor. I'm just worried that he will get his ass shot off." Keenan dashed for the door, the others right behind him.

Outside, the wind had dropped along with the temperature. As the group burst into the clearing outside the lab, Keenan heard the high whine of the glider's tiny motor. The sound was disappearing in the direction of the castle.

"Your friend has gone flying, again," Kron observed, holding up the glider's empty carrying bag.

"I think he's gone nuts," Chan speculated.

"I know where he's gone," Keenan replied. "I just have no idea why!"

As they stood looking up into the black sky, the five men remembered that they were outside in their skivvies and the temperature was hovering around freezing.

"Guys," Keenan said emphatically, "I am personally freezing my balls off out here! Let's get some gear on and we'll take turns waiting for the 'junior birdman' to come home."

"If, indeed, he comes home," Kron muttered under his breath. The five men hustled back into the warmth of the weapons lab.

The valley below was like a patchwork quilt done in grey and black. The whine from the glider's engine was unusually loud in the still night air, but he knew that it would be almost impossible to hear him on the ground. He shifted his weight and pushed the yoke to one side, turning the glider to a heading that took it directly away from the castle. He would gain altitude, then shut off the engine and glide over the fortress, snapping pictures with the small infrared camera.

"One pass and I'm out of there," he told himself. He would dive into the valley after the photo pass, circle around to lose altitude and go home.

The rush of wind on his face was icy, but it was more bracing than cold. His skin tingled and every nerve in his body seemed to be straining for more sensation. This must be how Jack feels all the time, he mused. I wonder if I could stand that.

There was a tiny altimeter on the glider's yoke, the kind skydivers wore on their wrists. The luminous red needle slowly inched its way around the dial as the glider climbed higher and higher into the dark sky.

A shiver, part cold and part thrill, ran through him as he watched the valley below grow smaller and smaller. Soon he would switch off the engine and glide silently over the castle. He smiled at the thought that he would literally be able thumb his nose at the dreaded Chairman Maximov himself.

Morgenau was yawning and stretching, waiting for the ancient coffee maker to spew out a few cups of what passed for coffee these days. When the machine gasped to a stop, Morgenau picked up the grimy pot and poured the evil-looking brew into his chipped china cup. In mid-pour, the radar alarm went off again.

Morgenau managed to slosh the hot stream on himself, narrowly missing his crotch. He dropped the pot onto the table top and dashed back to the machine. The alarm had been another weak, warbling sound, not a firm contact tone. The screen again seemed blank except for the ground clutter over the forest.

No, wait, he thought. Up in the top left quadrant was something new. It wasn't a blip, though, it was more of a smudge, a hazy little cloud that faded off the scope as he watched.

Templar's voice on the intercom made Morgenau jump. "Report!" the voice spat.

"Nothing, Herr Templar!" Morgenau answered. "The alarm went off, but there is nothing on the screen."

"I'm coming up!" Templar barked. The intercom went silent. Morgenau stepped quickly back over to the coffee pot and filled his cup.

I will need more than coffee to get through this night, he thought miserably.

When he was five hundred feet above the level of the fortress, Kinski turned the glider back toward the objective. He kept the engine on until he was nearly a thousand feet higher than the castle, then switched it off.

Even though the engine had been quiet, when he switched it off, the silence was profound. He could hear the rush of the wind across his face now, hear it singing through the glider's rigging. For a moment, he felt very fragile and afraid. What the hell was he doing up here on this kite, taunting the whole FSE? Crazy!

He took a couple of deep breaths. The dry, icy air chilled him and helped clear away the jitters.

"It's always this way before any mission," he pep-talked himself. "As soon as you get into it, you'll feel better." He concentrated on keeping the glider's sharp nose pointed toward the mountain which rose up like some malevolent tower from the dark valley.

"What is it, Morgenau?" Templar barked. Morgenau cringed inwardly.

"I don't know," he answered. "The alarm squawked a little bit, but there is nothing on the scope but ground clutter and an occasional weird blurring."

"When did you re-calibrate last?" Templar demanded.

"Last week," Morgenau answered.

"Re-calibrate now!"

"Yes, mein Herr!" Morgenau answered. Templar stomped out of room, but Morgenau doubted that he had seen the last of him for the night. He switched the machine to calibration mode and began to go through the long series of electrical tests that would bring the radar up to maximum performance.

"Bad coffee and bullshit," Morgenau commented. "What a life!"

He could see details on the castle fortress now, even in the dark. It was time to get the camera ready. Since this would be his only photo opportunity, Kinski hoped to swoop over the castle at about a hundred feet, snapping photos as fast as he could. He would have only seconds to get as many shots as the little camera could snap. Kinski shifted his weight a tiny bit to the side to balance himself with one hand. He snapped a few frames to make sure the camera was working, then concentrated on keeping the castle directly in front of him.

The old crenellated towers looked like broken teeth straining upward to bite him out of the sky and devour him. With a strong visual rush, the castle loomed up before him. Kinski held the camera to his face, peered through the viewfinder and pressed the shutter button. He could hear the camera whir and click as it snapped each shot.

The castle flashed below him and it seemed that the glider slowed in its flight. Kinski realized that the adrenaline surging through him was distorting time.

There was no movement below, but Kinski caught a glimpse of distracted guards leaning on the battlements, looking down toward the valley. Not one of them looked up to see him swooping over their heads. As he cleared the castle and swooped up on the draft off the side of the mountain, shooting a few final frames through his widespread feet, a Klaxon horn sounded behind him.

The fortress, dark and silent a second ago, was suddenly bright and alive. Two huge searchlights stabbed straight up at the dark sky and began to swing around in large circles, searching for him.

A big, twin-barrelled automatic gun fired a long burst behind him. Kinski heard the shells streak by. They sounded like huge, angry bees as they passed, their red tracers arcing out over the sleeping valley. He pulled the yoke close to him and shifted violently to the right, putting the glider into a steep, diving turn to the right. The searchlights swept the sky over him, but found nothing.

He hugged the side of the mountain, praying that no sudden wind shear would slam him into the unforgiving rocks only a few feet away.

When he was halfway around the mountain, he shifted his weight again, turning the glider out over the valley. He could not see above him, but the flurry of shooting had not abated. The searchlights still swept the sky high overhead. He had eluded them.

The glider began to shake and it took him a minute to realize that he was the source of the vibration. His hands, holding the yolk, were shaking like trip-hammers.

Morgenau finally completed the last calibration check. The machine was tuned as well as he could tune it. Considering its age, it was tuned as well as possible. He wiped the screen with a cloth to remove any smudges, then switched it over to SCAN.

A large solid blip appeared on the screen and the warning horn blared in his ear. He yelled in surprise, spinning to slam his palm onto the red alarm button on the wall next to the machine. Outside, the Klaxon sounded.

Morgenau watched the blip streak across the scope. In two seconds, the blip disappeared as if it had never been there. Behind him, the door burst open. The antiaircraft gun thudded outside, seeking the target that had already disappeared.

Morgenau looked back as his superior, his face wide-eyed and livid, lunged across the room, his eyes looked on the now-blank scope.

Morgenau watched as his young life passed before his despairing eyes.

NINETEEN

The wind had picked up a bit by the time he reached the clearing near the lab. Kinski had to rock the yoke back and forth to keep the glider into the wind as he settled in to land. The ground came up quickly and he took three fast running steps, tripped and fell to his knees as the glider nosed over. The yoke slammed into his stomach, knocking the wind out of him.

"Shit!" Kinski gasped, unbuckling the harness and dropping to the ground.

"You'll think 'shit' if you try a stupid stunt like this again," an angry, familiar voice snarled at him from behind. Kinski looked over his shoulder at Jack Keenan's glaring face.

"You want to share with us the purpose of this little nocturnal outing?" The big man railed on. Kinski struggled to his feet and dangled the camera in front of him.

"Pictures!" he wheezed. "I got pictures of the fort."

"It looks as if you got more than pictures," Mamudi commented. He and T'sinko were standing by the glider's wing tip.

Mamudi stuck his fingers up through two ragged holes in the fabric. "Looks like you came very close to getting a 23mm hemorrhoid-ectomy."

Keenan stepped forward and took the camera. He turned to T'sinko. "Can you develop this film?" Keenan asked, straining to keep his anger in check.

"Of course," T'sinko replied. "There is a small darkroom in the optic lab." He stepped over and took the camera from

Keenan. "I will go process it now," T'sinko said, looking sideways at Kinski. "It will take perhaps an hour." With that, the Russian disappeared into the darkness, leaving the Americans alone to discipline their errant flyer.

"Kinski, I ought to whip your ass," Keenan spat. "What a harebrained stunt!" Kinski slumped to the ground, rubbing his wounded arm, a hang-dog, pitiful look on his face.

"I thought we needed a recon," he answered by way of an excuse.

Mamudi, sensing Keenan's rising anger, stepped in. "That is quite valid, my friend," he said. "On the other hand, you were very nearly killed, and we may well have lost the element of surprise."

"We already lost the element of surprise!" Keenan snarled. "I'm pissed that you didn't bother to discuss this with me! Since when is this a solo act, huh? We're all fighting the same people, even those Russians in there!" Keenan sat down next to Kinski. The cold ground seemed to cool his temper a bit. "Besides," Keenan went on, "if you'd gotten shot down, we would've lost one of our tow planes. We wouldn't have been able to tow but one glider and you know how Freddie and Buddha fight over these little perks."

Kinski smiled. The ass-chewing was over, at least for now. The three men were silent for a moment.

"All right, come on," Keenan said, as he got to his feet. "Let's roll this baby up and go see those photos." He pointed a finger at Kinski's nose. "There better be some real film noir on that roll, or I may have to chew your ass again."

An hour later, the pictures were ready. T'sinko carried the still-wet prints out to the table and spread them out for all to see.

"You do not have a career as a photographer ahead of you," he said to Kinski, "but there are two or three excellent photos here."

The Russian was right. Most of the shots were blurred. One had two large blurs obstructing the frame. "My feet," Kinski explained.

One shot, though, taken directly over the fortress, was sharp. The infrared photo lacked the precise image of a regular photo, but the shapes of guns, searchlights, and even the warm bodies of the guards were clearly visible.

Kron and Mamudi, who had been repairing the bullet holes in the glider's wing walked over.

"What are these?" Mamudi asked, pointing at two long, thin structures set against the east wall of the fortress.

The two Russians exchanged glances. "If I am not mistaken," Kron suggested, "they are launch supports for the SS-NX-21 missiles."

"We trained on such targets," T'sinko explained, "before the war."

"You mean those are the missiles?" Kinski asked. "Damn it, I could taken them out while I was there!"

"No, my friend," Kron corrected him, "those are not the missiles. They are merely supports to hold the launch cannisters. The missiles must be inside."

"So, if we knock out these launchers, they can't launch the missiles?" Keenan asked, hopefully.

"I am afraid not," T'sinko replied. "The missile cannister is the real launcher. These are simply racks to hold the cannister in place. You must take out the missiles themselves."

"There is at least one positive fact," Kron pointed out. "The missiles are not on the launchers. They are not ready to fire them yet."

"Then we need to get our butts in gear before they are," Keenan growled. There was no argument. "How is that glider?" he asked Mamudi.

"Just about ready to go," Mamudi answered. "Kron claims to have been a rigger. He's pretty slick with that sewing needle." The short Russian grinned and the two men went back to their repairs.

Keenan turned to the now forgiven Kinski. "Pete, since you've been there, you can work out a flight plan for us." Kinski nodded. Keenan turned finally toward T'sinko. "Can you help us with some of this fancy hardware?"

"With pleasure!" the Spetsnaz officer smiled.

"How soon?"

Virograd fidgeted. "Two days, possibly three," he lied.

"No more than that!" the chairman snapped. "I want those missiles, and I want them soon!"

"Yes, Comrade Chairman," Virograd answered. "I am now testing the guidance systems. When I finish that, I will check the propulsion systems. Then the missiles will be ready to launch."

"See to it, Virograd," Maximov snapped again. "I am a patient man, but my patience is not unending."

"Exactly so, Comrade Chairman," Virograd answered as the phone went dead.

He looked at the two missiles resting on the long work benches. Out of their cannisters, the missiles were things of simple, awful beauty. Painted the same sky-blue color that had once graced Soviet interceptors, the missiles' appearance belied their terrible power.

He could feel that power every time he touched them. When he tested the various systems, he felt the urgency in the machines, their need to fly free and destroy.

He would miss them when they were gone, launched on their missions of death.

He walked over and ran his hand first down #9026, then down its companion, #9071, caressing their hard, curved flanks. He leaned down and put his cheek against the cold metal warhead.

"I will keep you near me as long as I can, my beautiful birds," he told the two flying city-killers. "Then you will be free to wreck the earth again, like the others before you."

After a moment, Virograd straightened up and walked back to the computer terminal nearby and turned on the small tape recorder on which he kept the record of his tests.

"Guidance sequencer test, #9071," he said as the computer brought the missile to life. The screen ran a column of numbers down the left side as a computer map came to life. Virograd felt the familiar thrill as the blue bird spoke to him again.

Rupert Morgenau sat at the hated console, watching the thin white line slowly sweep around the dark green screen. He rubbed the raw patch on his cheek where he had collided with the wall. His head still ached, but his swollen eye had gone down enough to see out of it again. His tongue played gently with the loose tooth up front. Hopefully, it would not come out. There was no dentist in the castle.

Morgenau was sure that Templar had bounced him off every flat surface in the room, except, of course, the precious radar console. He had lost consciousness, then awakened to slaps in the face and screaming. Later, one of the medical aides had told him that the whole castle had gone on alert and Templar had been called to the Commander's office to explain the false alarm.

Since then, Templar had been even less agreeable, if that was possible.

As Morgenau sat miserably watching the screen, his eyes focused upon the red light which indicated that the automatic warning horn system was on.

"That fucking warning horn is the cause of my troubles," he mused aloud. "Every time it goes off, that bastard Templar goes off, too."

An idea suddenly struck him. The horn must die!

A thin smile spread across Morgenau's split lips as he plotted the death of the hated horn. He ducked under the console, the motion making him dizzy for a second. There were the wires to the switch!

He pulled the connections loose and reversed the one leading to the red indicator light. This done, he carefully unscrewed the switch from the panel and reversed it. He switched off the automatic system. The light continued to glow as if the system was on.

Now only he would know if an intruder showed up on the screen! A feeling of relief swept over Morgenau. He had defeated his main enemy. Not the non-existent air forces of the rebels, but Templar, his supervisor and nemesis. Now he could live in peace for a while. Of course, if Templar learned of his ruse, it would be bad, but for now, this was a victory!

"Given your body weights and the lifting power of the gliders," T'sinko began, "we have selected the following equipment for your assault on the Schloss Adler."

On ponchos on the floor, T'sinko and Keenan had laid out an assortment of weapons.

"The two powered gliders will carry the heavier weapons and the unpowered gliders, the heavier people."

Keenan pointed at Buddha Chan. "That means you and me." Chan looked skeptical, but kept quiet for the moment.

"For heavy firepower," T'sinko went on, pointing to a thick green fiberglass tube on the poncho, "each man will have an

AT4 rocket launcher. It can stop a tank or open any door that might be locked."

He looked up and smiled slyly. "Think of it as a universal skeleton key." He next pointed to a pair of big cylindrical grenades on the poncho. "These thermite grenades will destroy the missiles, once they're found."

"Why not plastic explosives?" Mamudi interrupted.

"Because of the warheads," T'sinko answered. He took a piece of chalk and drew a quick sketch of the atomic warhead on the SS-NX-21.

"To destroy the warhead without detonating it," he explained, "you must set off the conventional explosives in such a way that they do not initiate the atomic explosion. Thermite grenades burn through the mechanism and set off the charges out of sequences. The warhead is destroyed, but does not detonate."

"What if we wanted to set it off," Kinski asked, "to, like, destroy the whole mountain?"

T'sinko looked solemnly at Kinski for a moment, then at the others. "Trust me, my friend," he answered. "You do not want to set off this device. It is small by nuclear standards, but it still awesomely powerful." He looked down at his feet for a second. "The radiation from a surface explosion on top of that mountain would make the area for twenty miles around uninhabitable for at least fifty years, possibly more, depending on the rainfall."

"Shit!" Kinski observed. Chan whistled softly through his teeth.

T'sinko continued his briefing. "Your personal weapons will be G-11 rifles with attached grenade launchers and one M249 machinegun. Each rifleman will carry six grenades and six magazines for a total of 300 rounds of ammunition."

"I'd rather carry my '14'," Chan interjected. "I trust it."

T'sinko looked at Keenan, who shrugged. "As you wish." He pointed to a strange-looking hand grenade on top of a flat nylon bag. "Here is my only other suggestion for you." He picked up the grenade. "This is an experimental tear gas. It causes uncontrolled weeping, panic and vomiting."

"Hey, Jack," Chan interrupted, "it's my ex-wife in a can!" The others chuckled, but T'sinko went on without a pause.

"It can break up a defense quickly, or cover an escape," he said. "You might consider it. Any questions?"

"Tell me more about this G-11," Mamudi said.

Kron hefted the small, boxy rifle as the Americans gathered around him. "It is simplicity itself," he explained. "The magazine snaps on here above the barrel. It feeds the ammunition back to the chamber here." He twisted a circular knob on the side of the rifle. "You cock it here, and it is ready to fire."

"And there aren't any empty cases?" Chan asked.

"None."

"It's a mean motor scooter," Kinski said, "and a bad gogetter!"

"It better be," Keenan cautioned. "It better be."

"So, Virograd," Maximov asked, "what have you got for me?"

"Comrade Chairman," the scientist answered. "The missiles have checked out and I have solved the launch problem. They are both ready to fire on your order."

"Excellent!" Maximov shouted. "You have done well, Virograd. You will be well rewarded!"

"I seek no reward, Comrade Chairman," Virograd assured him, "but I would ask a favor of you."

"Name it."

"I would like to be the one to actually pull the lever that fires the missile," Virograd asked. "If you please?"

Maximov laughed. "Indeed you shall, Virograd. That wish is gladly granted."

"Thank you, Comrade Chairman," Virograd said as the phone went dead. He turned and looked at the two missiles, now safely back in their launch cannisters.

"Soon you will fly, my pets," he crooned, "and the earth will tremble!"

"Probst!" Maximov barked. "Send your communications chief up here! I have a message to send!" Maximov hung up the phone without waiting for an answer.

"A message to King Shatterhand!" he said aloud. "An ultimatum to surrender or die!" Maximov shuddered as a near-sexual thrill ran through him. No one would refuse him now! He picked up a pencil and began to draft the message to his enemy.

He was finished when the radio officer knocked softly on the door.

"Come!" Maximov shouted. The officer entered his office, saluted and stood at rigid attention in front of the desk.

"I want this message sent on a frequency that the English use for their communication," Maximov ordered. "Repeat it until someone acknowledges it, or you know they have received it."

"Just so!" the radio officer snapped. Maximov waved him away.

Maximov smiled. The message was short but it left no room for confusion. He only wished he could be there when Shatterhand read it. That would be sweet indeed!

TWENTY

Donovan, the Signals Chief, knocked quietly, then walked in and laid the short message on the king's desk. Shatterhand read it, read it again, then looked up.

"This is all of it?" he asked.

Donovan nodded. "Yes, Your Grace," he replied. "They transmitted it three times to be sure we got it."

"Who else has seen this?" Shatterhand inquired.

"Only the radio operator, myself and you, Your Grace," he answered, "No one else."

"Thank you, Donovan." The signalman saluted and left.

Shatterhand stood and looked out the window at the grey sky.

The message said simply: "Capitulate to the forces of the FSE within 48 hours or suffer mass destruction. Radio your compliance on this frequency. Do not disregard this order. Maximov."

A radio frequency followed.

"So it's come?" he asked the overcast heavens. "God save us now." He paused for a second and added, "And God save those four good men who died trying to prevent it."

"Okay, one more time," Keenan said. He nodded at Mamudi.

"We take off from the knoll and fly east to gain altitude." Mamudi began the sequence, then passed it to Chan.

"Then when we get up above the castle, we loiter until the sun starts to come up," Chan continued.

127

Kinski took up the narrative next. "We attack from the east," he recited. "Freddie and I land the gear while you and Buddha work over the defenses."

Keenan took up the plan. "Once we're on the ground, we go after the missiles." He went on, "We strap the thermite grenades on the warheads, burn 'em till they pop, then back out and escape."

"By using the gliders, if possible." Mamudi jumped in.

"Or by the cable car," Chan added.

"Or by rope down the mountain," Kinski concluded, "if all else fails."

T'sinko and Kron stood by, waiting their turn. When Keenan looked over at them, Kron took up the briefing.

"We will cover your escape by staging a diversion against the garrison."

"While the garrison tries to deal with us," T'sinko added, "you can escape. Afterward, you will come back here."

"Right!" Keenan said. "Well, I guess it's time to get a little sleep, we have a busy day ahead tomorrow!"

The others nodded, knowing that there would be little sleep for anyone. They would rest, but sleep before a battle was impossible. The two Spetsnaz wandered off to check their equipment again as the four Americans retired to their bunks.

As he lay pretending to sleep, Keenan could feel the tension in the other three Marauders. From Kinski, he felt an intense excitement, the desire to begin an adventure. Chan radiated a kind of joy at rubbing the enemy's nose in his plan, the desire to ruin his desires. Only Mamudi seemed at peace. His faith assured him that if he died, he would ascend to heaven as a martyr. Keenan sensed no desire in Mamudi to achieve that status, just a quiet contentment.

And what did he feel? Keenan wondered. He searched his mind for the core of his feeling. Not anger, no, something stronger. Hatred. He hated the bastards that ruined the land, killed the innocent and now threatened to scorch the earth with nuclear fire again.

The bastards had to die! There could be no negotiations with them. You cannot negotiate with terror, he reminded himself. That was what had gotten them into this brave new world to begin with!

There was only one answer to terror and aggression—fire

and cold steel! In a few hours, Maximov's goons would taste some of both!

With that idea to warm him, Keenan fell into a deep coma-like slumber.

"What are their chances?" Kron asked softly as he checked the AK another time.

"Bad," T'sinko speculated. "But they have little choice, really."

Kron wiped the BG-15 grenade launcher under the AK's barrel with an oily rag. The two men sat in silence for a moment, working on their weapons with the easy familiarity that comes from years of experience.

T'sinko broke the silence. "Still, it would be a bonus if they could kill that reptile Maximov. The FSE would disintegrate without him at its head."

"Maybe it would be worth turning this valley into a nuclear burnout if it meant the end of the FSE," Kron speculated. T'sinko nodded.

"If they are not successful," he said softly, "perhaps we will have to consider it ourselves."

"Remember," Kron reminded him, "you are the one who made us both promise that we would never use them!"

T'sinko looked at his short friend. "That was before the FSE swine had any atomic weapons!" He took a deep breath, then sighed deeply. In addition to the weapons lab, they had been assigned another target during the brief war. They had not shared with the Americans that other target.

Fifty kilometers away, there was a small underground weapons storage bunker that held ten atomic devices small enough to be carried in a backpack. Those weapons were still there, waiting. The two Soviets had hidden the site and had not returned.

"I hoped that we would never see atomic weapons again, but here they are."

"Pandora's box!" Kron observed. "Once opened, the evil cannot be contained."

T'sinko laughed softly.

"Speaking of Pandora's box," Kron said brightly, changing the subject, "when this is over, why don't we dress up like farm hands again and visit Frau Essen's house of ill repute.

I could use an oil change after all this excitement!"

"Good idea, Comrade Senior Sergeant," T'sinko agreed. "If we're still in one piece, we will treat ourselves to a piece!"

On that lighter note, they began to pack their big rucksacks with the lethal load they would use on the FSE later that morning.

It looks like a play, Virograd thought as the missile cannister was lowered onto the launch rack. The bright searchlights, usually pointed upward in anticipation of air attack, were turned downward now to illuminate the installation of the two missiles. Joy welled up in him like water from a spring as the first long tube settled onto the rack, pointed westward. The voice from behind startled him.

"So, Virograd," Maximov boomed, "a triumph, yes?"

"Indeed, Comrade Chairman," Virograd groveled, "a great triumph for you over the enemies of the Federation." Maximov was smiling like a new father.

Below, the second missile was being gently lowered onto its rack. The first missile was now covered with an awning to shelter it from the elements. Even though its cannister provided more than adequate protection, Virograd had ordered the canvas awnings to safeguard his fledglings.

"In a few moments," Maximov crowed, "my power, that is, the power of the FSE, will be unchallenged!" Virograd heard the slip but pretended not to.

"Where is the launch station?" Maximov asked. Virograd pointed to a small rectangular metal shed a few feet behind and above them.

"There, Comrade Chairman."

Maximov frowned. "So close to the launch racks?" he inquired. "Will you not be burned by the rocket blast?"

"Not at all, Comrade Chairman," Virograd smiled. "The missiles are ejected from the cannister by compressed air. Their rocket motors fire after ejection. Thank you, though, for your concern."

As if you had any concern, Virograd thought to himself. You're only concerned about getting the missiles launched, not anyone's personal safety. You wouldn't care if I had to stand behind them and light them with a match.

The second missile was nestled in its rack now, and the

crew was erecting the canopy over it. The searchlights winked off, plunging the west wall into darkness. Only the crew's twinkling work lights lit the missile area now.

"Comrade Chairman," Virograd said cautiously, "if I might ask, when do you plan to fire them?"

Maximov fixed the rocket scientist with a stare that froze the thin marrow of his bones.

"I may never fire them, Comrade Virograd," Maximov answered, an edge of hostility in his voice. Virograd cowered beneath the Chairman's baleful gaze. Suddenly, Maximov's face was split by a wide grin. He clapped Virograd on the back, almost knocking the wind from him.

"But if I do, you will be the first to know about it, eh?" With that, the Chairman walked away, humming happily to himself.

Virograd managed a wan smile, wishing to heaven he had never asked something that was none of his business.

The foreman of the work crew reported that his work was finished. Virograd dismissed him and stepped up to the launch racks to make sure his instructions had been followed. He checked the electrical connections and the compressed air fittings. For once, everything was perfect.

He climbed the short ladder to the launch station and opened the metal shutters. The launchers were right below him. Beyond them, the valley stretched away far below. The sight thrilled him. When the time came, he would open the valves and pull the big lever that would inject the compressed air into the cannister.

The missile would burst forth over the wall of the fortress, its engine igniting as it unfolded its thin wings. Then it would streak away toward the enemy's city and bathe it in the fire of the sun. Their hateful king would be incinerated. Their pretentious cathedral would crumble. Their foul Thames River would boil!

Thinking of that exquisite moment made Virograd ejaculate.

"Well, are we ready?" Keenan asked as he strapped the thin harness on and tightened the straps firmly against himself.

"If we're not," Chan asked, "do we have to go anyway?"

Keenan smiled and nodded. "That's affirmative!"

"Then I guess we're ready!"

The takeoff would be the tricky part. The powered gliders would take off first from the small knoll. As the towline played out, Keenan and Chan, in the towed gliders, would take a short run off the side of the knoll to get their gliders moving. When the slack ran out, the powered gliders would pull them along behind. It was a simple plan, the kind that so often blows up in your face.

Mamudi and Chan were first up at bat. Kinski started the tiny motor as Keenan checked the coiled tow line.

"Pete," Mamudi shouted over the whine of the engine, "are you sure this will work?" Kinski smiled and patted the zipper-like scar on the little Afghan's face. Mamudi was wearing his black fiberglass stealth eyeball.

"Trust me!" Kinski said. Mamudi said something he couldn't hear for the engine noise, but Kinski didn't ask. He stepped back, gave Mamudi a thumbs-up and pointed down the knoll. Mamudi paused for a second to murmur a quick prayer to Allah, then gunned the little engine and ran down the slope. A few steps later, the glider took to the air. Mamudi pushed the yoke away from him, and the glider began to climb.

Chan was nervously watching the rope as the coils sprang up into the air after the tow glider. When about twenty feet were left, Chan hefted the glider and ran. What he lacked in grace, he made up in power. The glider lifted off seconds before the tow line went taut and jerked Chan along.

Kinski held his breath as Chan forgot to push forward on the yoke and nearly slammed into the trees. At the last second, Buddha remembered his flying lesson and soared up behind Mamudi's glider.

Now it was their turn. Keenan was already holding his glider off the ground, waiting for Kinski.

"Well, Air No-See-Um is off on its maiden flight," Kinski said with cautious optimism.

"Its only flight, I hope!" Keenan answered.

Kinski started the motor on his glider, slipped under the weapons bundle tied above him on the glider's frame, and buckled in. He turned to Keenan to give him a thumbs-up signal.

Keenan returned the gesture. Kinski opened the throttle. He could feel the tug of the engine, trying to push the glider aloft. Kinski took a deep breath.

"Here goes nothing," he said as he hefted the glider and ran off down the slope.

He woke up when his head hit the screen.

"Ahh!" Morgenau exclaimed, jerking himself bolt upright in the chair. The screen was clear. He twisted his head around toward the door. It was closed. Templar had not caught him sleeping.

"If that asshole would help watch the screen himself," Morgenau muttered, "I could sleep like a normal human being."

Since his big fuck-up, he was on 24-hour duty. Templar had blamed the whole thing on him, rather than on the worn out equipment. The man was a total ass-kisser!

Morgenau stood, shook himself, and walked over to the dingy coffee maker.

"Maybe some of this alkaloid desolation will help me stay awake," he sighed, pouring himself a cup of the acrid black liquid.

Standing at the coffee pot, his back to the console, Morgenau didn't see the strange pair of blips that skirted the side of the screen, headed east, away from the castle. As he stirred the strong liquid, the blips faded from the scope. His wiring project had been quite successful. The warning bell was silent. When Morgenau returned to the scope, it was clear. He settled into his chair, sipping the hot coffee.

TWENTY–ONE

Below them, the valley's dark fields shrank as they gained altitude. The air was cold but the four flyers took no notice of it except for the vapor that trailed behind them with each breath.

Mamudi had made one long circle waiting for Kinski and Keenan to launch. Now the two pairs of gliders flew together, Kinski leading. They flew east, gaining altitude slowly in the cold, dense air.

Kinski could feel the unsteady tug of Keenan's glider. The big redhead was trying the controls of his glider, shifting first one way, then another to get the feel of flying it. Off to the side, Chan and Mamudi were holding steady, unwilling to risk any maneuvering. Kinski prayed that their short training class had taught them enough to get them down in one one piece.

Dawn was a thin pink sliver on the horizon when Kinski motioned for Mamudi to follow him. He put the glider in a long, slow turn. In moments, the valley stretched before them, a grey carpet that led to the sinister tower that was the Schloss Adler.

There was still a stain on the floor where Kilnikov had been killed. Walter Ospenskiy eyed the dark patch as he wrapped his hands around the hot cup. There also was still a sticky spot on the bottom of the counter that had escaped the hasty

cleanup after the attack. He tried to ignore it, but his eyes kept
darting over to the spot. Kilnikov's head had been up against
the counter when they found him.

The hot tea did little to dispel the chill that ran through him.
It could as easily have been him here instead of Kilnikov. At
least he had not been at the upper terminal. Sgt. Krupke had
gone up to help fix the cable. His description of the wrecked
terminal and the massacre there had gotten everyone's attention. Guarding the Schloss Adler had been easy duty until
this week.

The intercom squawked beside him.

"Passengers coming down!" Hauser, the new officer in
charge, barked. Overhead, the big wheel began to turn as the
cable car descended from the castle. There was a vibration in
the cable that had not been there before. Ospenskiy was no
engineer, but he could feel the change and hear a different
whine in the sound the wheel made as the cable moved.
Considering how much damage it had endured, it was a
wonder that it worked at all.

T'sinko watched the cable car descend from the castle toward
the brightly lit terminal. The terminal was fortified now with
sandbags and a ring of razor wire strung on big wooden
X-shaped barricades. There was always a platoon on guard
now, after their previous attack.

T'sinko used his pocket binoculars to scan the dark river
beyond the terminal. From the small window, he could see
Kron working his way up the riverbank, the rocket mine on
his back. The mine was a new version of an old tank killer
that they had found in the lab. It was designed to shoot from
the side of the road at a passing tank. The new version was
radio controlled, fired by a small transmitter the size of a pack
of cigarettes.

Kron would set it up in the bank, so it would fire at the
cable car terminal on his signal. Hopefully, the troops guarding
the terminal would think they were under attack from that
direction.

T'sinko had an M249 Squad Automatic Weapon set up
in the window of the tiny storeroom, aimed at the terminal.
He had linked together 1500 rounds of the belted 5.56mm
ammunition. The belt was stacked on the table next to the gun.

Over the SAW's barrel, a two-quart canteen hung suspended from a length of parachute cord.

After Kron's rocket fired, T'sinko would tie down the trigger on the gun and open the canteen cap a bit so that a trickle of water would drop onto the gun barrel, cooling it as it fired up the belted ammo. By the time the gun ran out of shells and quit, he would be out of the building and gone.

He and Kron had stashed a variety of weapons in the village during the night. They would stir up as much trouble as possible to distract the fortress's defenders on the ground, then vanish as they had so many times before.

As he watched, the car began to descend from the castle above. He trained the binoculars on the swaying car. Inside, a group of women laughed and smoked cigarettes.

He wondered if they would be out of the terminal before the excitement started. If not, well, too bad.

The Schloss Adler loomed large before them as the first rays of the sun caught the turrets and bathed them in a warm pink light. They were half a mile out now, beginning their final descent on the castle. The missile launchers, covered by some type of awning, were clearly visible on the far wall. The missiles themselves must be nearby. They would set down on top of the launchers and go from there. Kinski looked over at Mamudi, who waved and pointed down. Kinski nodded in agreement.

He pulled the yoke back toward his chest. The glider's nose dipped, and the wind noise whistled a bit louder as they dropped toward their rendezvous with Maximov's missiles.

Morgenau was thinking about his home in Köln. The city had survived the war, and his family's home was still intact. He could just see his mother in the kitchen, fixing some sort of breakfast for his father and brother before they went to work at the foundry. Even when there had been nothing, she had always found something to feed them.

How he wished he were in that warm kitchen rather than here in this hellish fortress stuck atop a rock only slightly harder and more unforgiving than the people who lived there.

He stood and bent over, touching his toes and stretching. The motion was a mistake. His head spun for a second. Morgenau had to grip the chair to keep from falling.

Concussion, he remembered. I've got a concussion. He turned the chair and slumped against it as the spinning subsided.

Behind him, the two hazy patches rose up from the ground clutter and crept unseen across the screen.

Jack Keenan watched as Kinski gave him the cutoff signal. He reached up and pulled the simple latch that held the tow rope from his glider to Kinski's.

The taut rope snapped away and Keenan's glider suddenly slowed. For a second, he felt a rush of fear that the damn thing would fall out of the sky and slam him into the rock wall below the fort.

The glider dipped, picked up a little speed and soared on. Kinski's glider was ahead and above him.

Off to the left, Mamudi and Chan were doing the same. Separated from their tow planes, Keenan's and Chan's gliders suddenly developed a life of their own.

Keenan, with his heightened senses, could feel even slight changes in the glider's balance and shift his weight to compensate. Chan, on the other hand, threatened to go out of control any second. His glider's nose constantly rose and fell, swooped right and left and hung poised on the stall point.

"Easy Buddha," Keenan whispered. "You can't beat that baby into submission. Easy does it!" The castle was close now, spreading out on either side of him. He aimed the nose at the covered missiles and began to push slowly forward on the yoke to lose speed and settle on the wide, flat roof behind the missiles.

The edge of the wall was just ahead when his glider suddenly pitched upward, soaring high over the wall. Cursing, Keenan fought to get his glider under control. He pushed forward hard and realized instantly that he had made a mistake. The glider shuddered, slowing to a standstill. He was still high, maybe twenty feet up. He yanked back on the yoke and the nose dropped, but it was too late. Robbed of its speed, the glider lost its lift and dropped to the courtyard below.

Keenan watched the flat stones coming up beneath him and braced for the shock. It was not long in coming. He slammed into the rock floor, the glider knocking him flat. His breath whooshed out of him as pain flooded his overloaded senses.

As blackness closed in on him, he heard the distant honking of a Klaxon horn.

"No," he muttered, "not now!" The limp glider collapsed over him as Jack Keenan passed out.

Morgenau rubbed his face and pulled himself back up into the chair. The dizzy spell had passed. Morgenau glanced at the scope. Four large blips covered the entire right side of the scope.

He squeezed his eyes shut tight for a second, then stared at the scope. They were still there, closer now. Panic gripped him. Templar would know that the warning signal had not rung. He would kill him! For a moment, Morgenau thought about running for it, but there was nowhere to run to. He was trapped on this rock for better or worse.

The four blips were certainly worse. Morgenau slammed his hand against the alert button. Outside, the Klaxon screamed to life again.

Shaking, Morgenau stepped to the intercom panel, switched it to broadcast, and shouted into the microphone slots.

"Air attack!" he shouted. "East side! Repeat, air attack, east side!" He switched off the intercom and went back to the panel. The blips were now a large blob right over the center of the screen. Whatever they were, they were here now.

Morgenau switched the scope to long range scan to see if these intruders had any friends further out. The scope had hardly made one sweep when the door flew open and Templar stormed in.

"You little fuck!" Templar began. His remarks were interrupted by a loud boom that shook the room. Templar looked up in time to get a trickle of dust in his face from the ceiling.

"Ahhh!" he screamed, rubbing at his eyes. He wiped away the dust and then looked at Morgenau with a mixture of fear and hatred that chilled Morgenau to the bone. Before the frightened radar operator could answer, Templar bolted from the room. Morgenau realized that whatever else happened this morning, he knew who his worst enemy was.

When the updraft hit his glider, Kinski reacted by pulling up slightly and turning to catch the draft. He soared upward, cursing himself for not expecting the updraft from the mountain. He had failed to warn the others. As he turned, he saw the others fighting their gliders. He saw one stall over the courtyard, falling and crashing. A horn blared from the castle.

Mamudi's glider was soaring over the castle, missing the landing spot completely as it swept over the far side out of sight. Kinski reached up for the little engine's ignition. He switched it on, hoping he had enough speed to turn the little prop enough to start it.

Relief flooded him as he heard the little engine sputter to life. He gunned the motor and pulled the glider up in a tight turn back toward the fortress. As he turned he saw the crew of one of the twin 23mm antiaircraft guns swing the gun around. The team leader was pointing at the downed glider in the courtyard.

"Hello, fuckers!" Kinski shouted. "I'm back!"

He reached up and pulled the safety on the LAW rocket next to him. He pointed the glider at the gun position. The gun swam into his sights. As it crossed the scribed lines, he pressed the firing bar. The 66mm rocket burst from the tube, burning his face with its rocket blast. Kinski watched the rocket slam into the wall behind the gun.

The gun crew died in a cloud of black smoke and whining steel. Kinski cut the throttle as he swept over the edge of the wall, pushing slowly forward on the yoke as he crossed over the courtyard. He dropped onto the stones at a run, slowing the glider. He had misjudged a bit. The nose slammed into a door on the far wall, slamming it shut in the face of a wide-eyed FSE soldier.

Kinski unclipped himself from the frame and unbuckled the weapon bundle above him, catching it as it fell into his arms.

He ducked under the collapsed glider as a stream of bullets from the wall ripped through it. He swung the G-11 off his shoulder and fired it one-handed as he ran for the wrecked glider in the middle of the courtyard. The little rifle roared, but hardly kicked at all.

A flash from the wall revealed the shooter as the stones around him chipped and whined. Kinski jerked the barrel over and fired the grenade launcher. A section of the wall came loose as the grenade wiped out the enemy rifleman.

Shots rang out from higher on the castle walls. The familiar booming of AKs was met by the flat crack of an M14. Chan had made it down, at least. Still it didn't look promising. Air No-See-Um was turning into another Lockerbie.

From his window, T'sinko saw the glider swoop over the edge of the castle. The Americans were attacking. As he dropped his binoculars, he saw the flash of Kron's rocket as it fired toward the ground terminal. He unscrewed the cap on the canteen to start the water flow. As the cold water splashed down on the gun barrel, T'sinko pinched open the metal clip and slipped it over the trigger. The gun roared to life as he released the spring on the clip. T'sinko watched the stream of tracers as he walked the fire onto the terminal building. When he was locked on target, he picked up the sandbag and set it over the gun to keep it in place. This done, he ran for the door as the machine gun spent itself against the cable car terminal.

Ospenskiy watched the cable car slow as it approached the terminal. He could see the passengers better now. They were all girls! Not just girls, either. Tarts. Their low-cut gowns and garish makeup looked cheap and tawdry in the early morning light. They were laughing as the car docked in the terminal.

He stepped over to open the door. Cheap or not, they were lookers. They smiled teasingly at him as they stepped from the car and stood somewhat uncertainly in the terminal.

One of them, a striking black-haired girl with a wide expanse of milk-white cleavage threatening to burst from her tight, strapless dress, walked over to him.

"Are there no autos for us?" she purred. He was mesmerized by her pale blue eyes, not to mention her substantial breasts. He shook his head.

"You mean we have to walk home?" she spat, her tone changing from a purr to a snarl. She grabbed the top of her dress, which made her breasts jostle in a way he could hardly bear to watch. "We'll freeze to death in these!"

"I'm sorry," he stammered, "I don't know if you . . ." His apology was interrupted by a roaring noise that turned into an explosion. The empty cable car disintegrated in a ball of orange fire. Two of the women spun to the floor like rag dolls. The angry brunette in front of him gasped and fell into his arms, her beautiful eyes wide with fear and confusion. As Ospenskiy caught her, he could feel the warm wetness on her back where metal had ripped through her thin dress. The two of them sank to the floor. Ospenskiy held the girl until her body went limp and her blue eyes stared up at a world he could not see, but soon might. Out front, machine guns rattled to life. The glass windows shattered as bullets whined into the terminal. Smoke filled the room.

The girls who had survived the blast were screaming now, clawing their way along the floor toward the dubious safety outside. Ospenskiy gently laid the dead girl on the floor, kissed her quickly on the lips, closed her dead eyes, then crawled back to the counter for his weapon.

Keenan was out cold, but stirred as Kinski unclipped his harness and dragged him out from under the wrecked glider.

"Come on, Jack!" Kinski urged. "It's you and me against the world, buddy. I need some help!" Hot slugs skipped off the stones around them, whining like angry hornets. Keenan was fighting to wake up; stumbling and making loud guttural sounds as he tried to push away the black lace curtains around his mind.

Kinski dragged him into a doorway as bullets began to whine all around them. Chan's weapon was still firing, closer now, but there seemed to be no escape from the narrow doorway. Kinski tried the heavy wood door. It was locked from the inside.

"Move, Jack!" Kinski shouted, pushing Keenan around the corner and following him.

Kinski grabbed Keenan's rifle off his shoulder, thrust his own rifle into Keenan's hands, stuck the borrowed rifle around the corner and pulled the grenade launcher trigger.

The 40mm grenade exploded, blowing the door inward off its hinges. Kinski pulled Keenan around the corner after him, seeking safety in the corridor beyond the now open door.

He was barely around the corner when the corridor erupted with muzzle flashes and the roar of AK's. Kinski threw himself back against Keenan and pulled the now nearly conscious man down beside him.

"Looks like I got us right between a rock and a hard place," Kinski cursed. "Wake up, Jack, I need you!"

"Thanks, Pete, I love you, too," Keenan said behind him. Kinski heard Keenan reload the grenade launcher on his rifle. "Here, give 'em another one of these," Keenan suggested. As they swapped rifles again, more shots glanced off the stone wall. Keenan turned and sprayed the walls around the courtyard. Several screams spoke of his success.

Kinski jammed the barrel of his rifle around the corner and fired the grenade launcher again. A loud boom followed the shot, accompanied by more screams from the corridor. From inside, more firing erupted. It was as if the grenade had only angered the defenders. A heavy machine gun added its steady roar to the din.

"We're fucked, Jack," Kinski shouted. "We need fire support now!"

"It's coming," Keenan shouted. He pointed up toward the castle wall. Mamudi's glider swept up over the wall. Keenan swept his arm toward the corridor, his finger pointing at the target. Mamudi dropped the glider's nose and fired the LAW rocket strapped next to his head.

The rocket flashed out of the tube and streaked down the corridor. A huge crash followed. Smoke and flame belched out of the corridor. Keenan and Kinski both lunged around the corner and fired long bursts into the inferno. They turned as a dark shadow fell over them.

Mamudi flared out and landed the glider almost on top of them like some spectral bat out of hell.

"Nice of you to drop in," Kinski snapped. "Where you been?"

"I was admiring the scenery on the far side of the mountain," Mamudi answered as he quickly unclipped himself from the harness. "You failed to mention the air currents near the wall!"

"Sorry about that," Kinski whined.

"Did you see Buddha?" Keenan asked.

"Yes," Mamudi answered. "He's putting on a firepower demonstration up on the wall."

"You go support him!" Keenan ordered. "We're good here."

"I do not think that will be necessary," Mamudi said. "Chan will be here soon, I think."

Mamudi's observation was drowned out by a flurry of shooting on the wall just above their heads. As the three ducked close to the stones, two riddled FSE soldiers dropped onto Mamudi's glider.

"That will be him now," Mamudi predicted. A moment later, the Mongol sniper's voice rang down from above them.

"Quit hiding down there and help me kill these bastards," he suggested.

"On our way, Buddha," Keenan shouted.

The alert horn scared Virograd out of the sweetest dream he had ever had. In his dream, Chairman Maximov stood beside him and begged him to fire the missiles to save the FSE from total destruction by the rebels and their English friends. He stood God-like behind the console and pulled one lever, then the other. His magnificent birds had streaked off to the cheering of the army massed below him. Maximov had been crying as the dream had abruptly shattered. The hollow boom of explosions made his skin crawl as he leaped out of bed, still only partly awake.

A sudden terror gripped him. The missiles! They were surely the target of this attack. He struggled into his clothes, grabbing his jacket as he bolted through the door.

He ran down the corridor and up the stairs toward the control room and his precious endangered birds.

Yevgeny Maximov was shaving when the horn blared.

"Damn!" he cursed as the straight razor cut a long, thin line across his throat. His own men had nearly accomplished what his enemies longed to do. He was wiping the blood and shaving soap from his neck when the first explosion shook his room.

This is not possible, he thought, wiping the red slash on his throat. An hour ago I was screwing that little black-haired doll, now I'm under attack! It's not possible!

Another series of explosions affirmed that, possible or not, it was happening.

"The missiles," he blurted. "They're after the missiles!"

He pulled on a shirt and trousers, running for the door. Maximov was halfway down the hall before he realized that he was barefooted. The sound of small arms fire chattered, punctuated by the sharp bangs of grenades.

Outside, one of Probst's captains was trying to rally a group of frightened soldiers. Maximov grabbed the man.

"The missiles!" he screamed, pointing at the west wall. "Protect the missiles!" The captain nodded and began grabbing the confused troops by their jackets and pushing them toward the missile racks.

Maximov cautiously peeked over the wall. In the courtyard, a strange fabric contraption lay crumpled on the flat stones. A firefight was in progress, but he could not see the enemy. Probst's troops were pouring fire into an alcove at one side of the courtyard.

Maximov watched, stunned, as a dark shape swept up over the west wall and fired a rocket into the alcove. The dark machine, a glider of some sort, swooped into the alcove right behind the rocket as Maximov watched mystified.

A squad of troops was running along the wall above the alcove. Maximov smiled. They would get the invaders! His smile turned into a look of horrified amazement as the squad suddenly pitched and writhed as bullets ripped into them. A short, ugly man in black fatigues ran to the edge and called down to the other invaders. When the black-clad man trained his gun on the wall and fired a long sweeping burst that worked its way toward him, Maximov ducked behind the stones. The bullets whined loudly as they ricocheted off the wall.

There was only one group insane enough to attack him here, and tough enough to survive.

"Marauders!" Maximov cursed. Then he smiled. They would not get away from him here! They were as trapped as he was, and he had an army to back him up. The Marauders were as good as dead!

Virograd's hands shook as jabbed at the lock with the key which hung around his neck. He finally managed to get the key into the padlock and twisted it. The lock fell open. Virograd lurched inside, slamming the door closed. He dropped the heavy bar that locked the room from the inside. Amazingly, the missiles were fine.

Virograd switched the missile arming panel on. As it warmed up, he twisted the valves atop the compressed air bottles behind him. Outside, the sound of gunfire increased. For the first time, Virograd felt personal fear. He had never been around guns.

They were loud and heavy, and he had never liked them. He suddenly wished he had one.

His missiles were the most powerful weapons on earth, but they wouldn't do him much good against some barbarian with a bayonet.

Virograd jumped as someone banged on the door.

"Virograd!" the Chairman's voice shouted through the sheet metal. "Let me in!"

"Immediately, Comrade Chairman," Virograd shouted. He lifted the heavy steel bar. The Chairman, barefooted and wild-looking, nearly knocked him down as he jumped into the room.

"Prepare your missiles for launch!" Maximov shouted. Virograd had never seen the man so agitated before. Usually, the Chairman was the picture of calm arrogance. This morning, he looked like an escapee from a mental institution.

"I have already begun launch procedures," Virograd assured the man. "All I await is your order to fire."

"Excellent," Maximov shouted. "Remain here until I order you to stand down!"

"Yes, Comrade Chairman!" Virograd answered.

The chairman started to leave then turned back to him. "Take your orders only from me," he ordered. "Do you understand?"

Virograd nodded vigorously. "Exactly so, Comrade Chairman!" he snapped. Maximov spun on his heel and disappeared. Virograd dropped the locking bar into place.

I understand, he thought, what you mean is that I cannot surrender to anyone. It was just as well. He would die before he let anyone else have the birds.

It only took a second to open the equipment bundles and load the weapons on their shoulders. Keenan was awake now and seemed to vibrate. He shouldered two AT4 launchers like they were match sticks and stuffed his shirt with frag and gas grenades.

"Leave some for the rest of us, Jack," Mamudi suggested. Keenan did not seem to hear.

"Mamudi, you and Kinski find a spot to cover Buddha and me," he barked. "Buddha, grab one of those AT4s. We're going bird hunting!"

Kinski grabbed at Keenan's shoulder. "Hey, we want in on this, too!"

"Sorry, Pete," Keenan rasped. "This job is tailor-made for a Marine. You make sure no one shoots us in the back!"

"OOH-RAH!" Chan observed as he snatched up the bulky launcher and started after his boss. "Semper Fi, Pete!" he called over his shoulder to the disappointed Kinski.

Keenan's senses were on high today. The concussion had jumbled them for a moment and he had been lost in a cloud of sound, smell, blurred vision, and pain that flashed from a hundred places on his body. That was all pretty well sorted out now. Ahead of them, Keenan could sense fear and confusion. The FSE was still reeling from their offbeat assault. They would strike before the defenders got their shit together.

"Cover me!" he shouted at Chan. The Marine sniper dropped prone; the long M14 in front of him.

"Go!" Chan spat.

Keenan dropped into a crouch and ran for the steps twenty meters in front of him. A helmeted head, then another, popped up in front of him from the low wall at the top of the stairs. He hardly had time to bring his weapon up before the helmet flew off one of the men as Chan put a 7.62mm through his head. The other defender glanced at his dead comrade. That glance cost him his life as Keenan walked a short burst up the wall and across the man's worried face.

Keenan twisted as he reached the stairs, slamming his back against the wall, his weapon searching the top of the stairs for more targets. There were none. He heard Chan scramble to his feet and run up behind him. Keenan motioned the Mongol ahead of him. Chan slowly ascended the stairs, his rifle trained on the top step. In a few seconds, he crouched on the top steps and waved Keenan up behind him.

"Where are they, Jack?" Chan murmured. "I got a bad feeling!"

Chan was right. He could feel the enemy all around them. They were massing for a counterattack, of that he was certain. But from where? A storm of firing off to the right answered his question.

A platoon, led by a young officer clad in boots, pants and a red undershirt, boiled around a bend in the stone walkway, firing wildly as they ran. Bullets whined and sparked around them as they shifted to engage the small horde.

Keenan hardly got a round off before the platoon was raked by fire from off to the left. Red tracers from the M249 stitched through the FSE platoon, dropping them like feed sacks. A grenade exploded, shredding others.

The young officer in red, oblivious to the slaughter behind him, charged the stairs, firing as he ran.

Chan shot the young man through the heart. He stumbled, dropped to one knee, and kept firing.

"Oh, man," Chan complained as he squeezed off another round that hit right above the red undershirt. The officer pitched backward, his weapon finally silent.

"That bastard had balls!" Chan growled. "I almost hated to shoot him." He looked up at Keenan's curious face. "Almost," Chan clarified.

The rest of the platoon had retreated back around the corner, out of the kill zone.

"Which way are the missiles?" Chan asked. Keenan pointed down the walkway.

"Over there, somewhere," he answered. Another flurry of firing broke out, showering them with rock chips. The FSE had regrouped and were hosing the walkway with blind fire from the corner.

"I'm open to suggestions," Keenan said, ducking the whining ricochets from the rock walls around them.

"I'm thinking," Chan offered. "What about the gas?"

Keenan nodded. "Excellent plan!" Keenan pulled a tear gas grenade from his shirt and hooked his finger in the ring. "Ready?" he asked.

"Go!" Chan shouted. As Chan fired three quick shots down the walkway, Keenan hurled the grenade toward the corner. It skittered across the stones, bouncing and twirling as it spewed grey smoke. It stopped ten feet from the corner.

"Damn!" Keenan spat, striking the wall next to him with his fist. "Not far enough!"

"Hang on," Chan suggested. He flipped the barrel of his rifle around the edge of the wall and fired again. The grenade shot forward, caromed off the wall like a cue ball and disappeared around the corner.

"Nice shot!" Keenan blurted. The best sniper in the corps just smiled.

"Of course!" he admitted modestly. The sound of choking and a few screams echoed around the corner. The light morning breeze was spinning the gas in a mini-whirlwind. The sound of retching reached them.

"Let's go before we get a whiff, too," Keenan suggested. Chan covered the red-haired giant as he bolted up from the stairs and down the walkway toward the missiles. A second later, Chan followed. There was no more firing from the unlucky platoon. They were busy blowing breakfast on the hard stones of the Schloss Adler.

As Probst emerged onto the parapet, fully dressed in his battle uniform, the firing grew louder. He was startled to see the Chairman of the FSE crouching there, half dressed, looking like an escapee from debtors' prison.

"Stop them!" Maximov screamed, lunging up at him. "They are after my missiles!"

Probst saluted, trying hard to keep any hint of a smile off his face. "I will do just that, Comrade Chairman."

Probst barked at the young captain, who turned and quickly gave his commander a report. Behind Probst, other troops were pouring out of the barracks. At Probst's command, the young captain separated the newcomers into sections and dispersed them to guard the missiles.

"From the bizarre type of assault and the small number of attackers," Probst explained to the agitated chairman, "I believe the attackers are the so-called Marauders."

"I know that!" Maximov screamed into his face. "I want you to kill them!"

"Of course," Probst answered. Another batch of troops poured out of the barracks.

"All of you," Probst bellowed, "come with me!" With that simple order, Probst took command of the men himself and moved off after the audacious men who had attacked his fortress.

Maximov watched Probst and his men disappear down the parapet.

"Fucking martinet!" he snarled at Probst's back. "Looks like a damn Prussian recruiting poster!" Maximov suddenly realized he was alone again and bolted off after the missile guards.

• • •

"I thought those fucking missiles were right over there!" Chan cursed. A burst of machine-gun fire pocked the stone wall behind which he and Keenan were crouched.

"They are," Keenan answered. "That's why those guys are so thick."

"What happened to our fire support?" Chan asked next. Keenan smiled.

"Are you nervous, Buddha?" he asked quietly. Chan looked up at his boss. Crazy Jack looked anything but crazy now. He had the calm self-assurance of a man totally at peace with himself and the world. He almost seemed to glow with confidence.

"Fuckin'-A, I'm nervous," Chan blurted. Keenan smiled.

"Look at it this way," he suggested. "The bastards can't get away from us this time!" Keenan laughed softly. The sound gave Chan the creeps.

This time, he thought, Jack's gone over the edge for sure.

A blast shook the wall, putting an end to Chan's speculation.

Kinski fired again with the M249. Two more of the choking men dropped to the stones and lay still.

"Those guys are so messed up, I feel bad about shooting them," he said softly to Mamudi, who was reloading his grenade launcher.

"Believe me," he reminded Kinski, "they would have no qualms about doing the same to you!"

"I guess so," Kinski answered, firing two short bursts that dropped three more men onto the pile dead FSE heroes. "Still, it's just like a turkey shoot!"

"Happy Thanksgiving," Mamudi replied as he fired another grenade into the swirling smoke cloud. Heavy firing broke out to their right.

"Looks like Jack and Buddha have found the goodies!" Kinski observed.

"Let's go help them!" Mamudi suggested.

"I'm with ya," Kinski agreed. "I've got a score to settle for Greta and her family!"

The two men shouldered the heavy AT4 launchers and ran back down the way they had come, following the sound of the guns.

• • •

Ernst Kruger struggled out of his bed. The sound of combat above him thumped and shook the stone walls of his room. His wounds had become infected and he had been sick with fever for days.

"You bastards!" he groaned as he struggled to pull on his clothes. "I'll pay you back for this!"

Once dressed, he sat in his chair gasping for breath. In a moment, he struggled out of the room, picking up the AKM in the rack next to the door. Using the wall for support, he staggered along, his hate and anger driving him forward.

"You sons of bitches, you hurt me!" he gasped. "Now I'll see you dead if it takes my last breath to do it!"

He stopped at the foot of the staircase that led up to the parapets, resting for the hard climb.

The fight will be over before I get there! he thought, looking up at the steep stairs. Kruger took a deep breath and began to pull himself up, one painful stair at a time.

TWENTY–TWO

The two invaders were trapped.

Probst's men had kept them pinned down as Captain Dubek's platoon moved around behind them. In a moment, Dubek's platoon would be the anvil against which Probst's force would hammer the two intruders to dust.

"Now, Comrade Chairman, you will see real soldiers at work," Probst whispered under his breath. A lookout from up on the parapet slithered down to Probst's side.

"Captain Dubek is in position!" he blurted. Probst drew his pistol, checked the magazine, and threw a round into the chamber.

"NOW!" he bellowed. Half of his company began a torrent of fire to keep the two invaders' heads down. The remainder moved quickly down the stone parapets to positions nearer the two men. From there, the entire force would assault across the roof on line.

The tracers arced off the stones sending red streaks in every direction like holiday fireworks. The sun, now well up over the horizon, lit the scene in a sharp yellow light that made everything seem hyper-real.

Probst's heart soared. It had been so long since he had a real fight!

The whine of ricochets began to sound like a dial tone.

"Jeez, Jack," Buddha complained, "they're taking this real personal!"

151

"No sense of humor, I guess," Keenan replied, snapping a new magazine into his G-11. There was a brief pause in the enemy fire, then it began again from a new direction.

Keenan could sense the enemy moving in front of them, shifting positions. Worse than that, he could sense somebody moving behind them as well.

"Buddha, I think those fellows are about to rush us!" he said, dropping a grenade into the G-11's launcher. "Put on your mask!"

As Chan jerked the rubber mask from the bag on his thigh and slipped it up over his head, Keenan pulled his remaining tear gas grenade from his shirt.

"Get your mask on, Jack!" Chan shouted, his voice muffled by the gas mask. "Remember the lab?"

"Too fuckin' well!" Keenan answered. One whiff of Rilchinski's gas had nearly killed him. Now, his heightened senses would never tolerate a strong dose of the tear gas.

As Keenan masked, Chan took out his two grenades. Overhead, the fusillade continued unabated.

Keenan felt a surge of excitement from the enemy to their front.

"Hang on, Buddha," he yelled. The firing suddenly slacked off, then began again, slower.

"Now!" Chan's grenade sailed up over the wall, popping in the air and trailing tear gas as it bounced and skittered past the line of men advancing along the roof above them. Keenan's grenade followed, dropping in front of the assault line.

Seconds later, the two Marauders heard the sound of coughing coming from the attackers. Chan threw his remaining grenade. The coughing increased as the volume of fire decreased from the attackers.

Keenan pointed down the wall, gesturing for Chan to move. The masked Mongol quickly duck-walked a few meters, then turned, waiting for Keenan's signal.

Keenan moved his G-11 to port arms, held up his fist to signal "ready," then jerked it down.

Both men stood and flipped their weapons up over the wall. Keenan fired his grenade at the center of the line, then raked the line of choking, gasping men with 4.7mm bullets that ripped pieces of flesh from them and blew dark crimson holes through their spasming bodies.

Chan was firing single shots from his M14. With each shot, another soldier slumped to the stones that now ran red with spilled blood.

As one soldier died in mid-vomit, Chan saw a tall man in battle fatigues shouting at the others and gesturing with a pistol.

"Hello, leader," Chan muttered as he placed the thin crosshairs on the tall man's chest.

The attack was unraveling.

"Forward!" Probst shouted. "Get in front of the gas."

A whiff of the pale grey gas passed by him. Probst felt his chest contract, trying to force the gas out. His eyes suddenly burned and his stomach turned over.

Vomit gas! Where had these maniacs found vomit gas? Probst shook off the nausea and willed himself forward. His assault line was wavering now. Many of the men were on their knees, heaving their guts out onto the stones. The stench of vomit mingled with the gas to bring others down.

"Forward!" Probst coughed. Ahead of them, shooting suddenly erupted. A sharp blast blew away the center of the line. His troops began to drop like flies, the smell of blood added to the stench. He tried to rally the remaining men as another tendril of the gas snaked around him filling his eyes with the acrid smoke.

The man in front of him fell.

"Charge!" Probst screamed. "Damn you, charge!"

A huge fist hit him in the chest, knocking the breath from him and slamming him onto his back. Probst gasped for breath, only to get a lungful of the hateful gas. He doubled up, convulsed and retched, the taste of bile flooding his mouth.

Probst clawed at the canvas bag on his hip, digging in it for the flare gun. The flare was the signal for Dubek's men to attack the invaders from behind. Now, only Dubek's anvil could save his broken hammer. Probst got the gun out, rolled on his back and fired. The red flare streaked up above him, trailing smoke.

As the black clouds rolled over him, Probst heard loud firing break out behind the invaders.

"Quickly, Dubek," Probst whispered, "quickly, before I die."

"We got 'em now, Jack!" Chan shouted. The assault seemed to have been broken by the gas. Without masks, the FSE troops were faltering, falling, and barfing their brains out.

The two Marauders were showing them no mercy. Keenan raked the line with burst after burst from his G-11. Chan took out another retching wretch with each shot. In a moment it would be over.

Both men looked up as a red flare popped overhead. Keenan looked at the bright signal, then dropped behind the wall.

"Get down!" he screamed at Chan. The Marine sniper dropped down just as a storm of firing broke out behind them. Bullets whined and cracked off the stones all around them. A burst climbed the wall next to Keenan, one of the slugs ripping the black sleeve of his jacket.

Keenan whirled, firing a burst that went high over the heads of the new enemy force.

"I think we're fucked, buddy," Chan yelled as he spun, searching for the source of the shots that ripped into the rocks all around them.

Keenan found it hard to argue with that theory. He dropped his last grenade into the launcher. However it came out, it would be over in a minute.

"Get down!" Mamudi hissed, dragging Kinski off his feet. A line of FSE defenders had leaped up, firing madly as they advanced. Off to one side, another bunch had set up a heavy barrage on the edge of a roof several meters ahead of them. Mamudi crawled forward to get a better look at the fight.

"It's Jack and Buddha!" Mamudi barked over his shoulder. "They're pinned down!" Kinski slithered up beside him. The line of FSE troops had paused to let their comrades catch up. Now the entire line was moving forward, firing at the roof edge. Tracers spun off in all directions. Several of them whined overhead.

"Oh, God" Kinski gasped. "Come on! We gotta help them!" Kinski started to rise, but Mamudi pulled him back. A pale grey gas was swirling around the attackers. FSE soldiers were dropping, some debilitated by the gas, some shot down.

"We will help them," Mamudi suggested, "but not by getting wasted ourselves. Give them some fire support from here."

"Right!" Kinski answered, popping out the bipod on the M249. He pushed the gun out in front of him and was lining up on the enemy when a red flare streaked up into the sky.

A whistle sounded from behind a wall just ahead of them. Suddenly a large group of FSE welled up on the parapet and began to fire at Keenan and Chan from behind. The frontal assault had stalled, but now Keenan and Chan were caught in a cross fire.

Kinski shifted up, bringing the barrel of his machine gun to bear on the mob of FSE now streaming out onto the parapet. He fired a long burst, working the stream of red tracers along the line of riflemen who were firing down at his two friends. The SAW's stream of 5.56mm slugs ripped along the enemy troops like a little red ripsaw.

Next to him, Mamudi was at work with his G-11. He fired a grenade at a group clustered nearby, then went to work with the rifle. The grenade had not even landed when his first burst brought down two FSE who were setting up an old PK machine gun.

It didn't take the FSE long to figure out that they were in a cross fire as surely as the men to their front. They whirled and began to return fire on the machine guns to their rear. Mamudi concentrated on these as Kinski continued to rip into the enemy firing at Chan and Keenan. One squad decided to return to their original covered position. Mamudi saw them disappear.

"I'll take care of them!" he yelled. "Keep on the others!" The thin Afghan rose to a crouch and ran down a set of stairs a few meters away.

Kinski kept up his fire on the others. A moment later, a grenade banged followed by a series of long bursts. The silence afterward told Kinski that Mamudi had been successful.

"The rest of you are mine!" Kinski shouted at the remaining FSE. They had lost all interest in their original targets and were now looking for some stone to put between them and the little machine gun that was cutting them down like wheat.

Virograd cringed in the corner of his control center. The shooting outside was louder now. Explosions punctuated the gunfire like loud exclamation points. Fear gripped him like the nuns had gripped him so many years ago when he had misbehaved in Catholic school.

The sudden pounding on the control room door frightened him so badly, his skin crawled. The Chairman's voice rang through the door.

"Virograd!" he screamed. "Let me in!" It took all of Virograd's courage to crawl over to the door and raise the bar. Maximov nearly tripped over him as he burst through the door.

"Get up!" the chairman screamed, reaching down and grabbing Virograd's arms. The chairman hauled the quaking scientist to his feet.

"We cannot wait!" Maximov shouted into Virograd's face. "We must fire them now!"

A sudden change came over Virograd. The man stopped shaking and stood up. A smile spread across his face, a smile that made Maximov step back. Virograd changed from a quivering mass of fear to a—what? A fanatic, Maximov decided. Virograd suddenly had the look of a martyr, a man unafraid of anything, death least of all.

Virograd stepped over to the launch console and began his launch countdown.

"We will be ready to fire in four minutes, Comrade Chairman," he said brightly. He looked over and gave Maximov a smile that made the chairman's blood run cold.

Outside, the firing was slacking off a bit. Maximov hoped that the lull meant that the damned Marauders were destroyed, but he knew from bitter experience that was not the way to bet.

The remaining FSE had died screaming and gagging in the lingering wisps of gas. Chan and Keenan had put a round into anything that moved on the roof in front of them. In a minute, nothing moved at all.

"Come on, Buddha," Keenan urged. "We gotta find those launchers!"

"Right behind you, Jack," the stocky Marine answered as Keenan vaulted over the wall and ran past the shattered remains of the assault line. He stripped off his mask as he ran, stuffing it into his shirt. He bolted across the roof and jumped up onto the wall behind it. Chan was right behind him, and the two men leapfrogged down the top of the castle's east wall, searching for the twin launchers.

Time dragged for Keenan as he searched with his eyes and with his heightened senses for the missiles. If they could not get to them in time, well, he didn't want to think about the consequences of that.

The whooshing of compressed air just ahead caught his attention. He flattened himself on the stones and scuttled forward to the edge of the wall.

Below and perhaps thirty meters ahead of him, the two launchers sat shaded by their canvas canopies.

"Bingo!" Keenan shouted back to Chan. He unlimbered the AT4 launcher as Chan quickly crawled up beside him. There seemed to be no one around the launchers to guard them.

"Let's take out the control room first, Buddha," Keenan said. "Then we'll go down and thermite the warheads."

"Roger copy," Chan answered. Both men pulled the safety wire from the base of the launcher. They pushed forward and to the right on the cocking levers and pulled the plastic covers back from the sights.

Keenan had the small control room in his sights when the first missile launched with a loud *Whoosh!* from its cannister.

"NO!" Keenan screamed, transfixed by the horror of the missile launch.

Propelled by the compressed air, the SS-NX-21 blew out of the cannister like a long blue cigar and dropped slowly toward the valley floor below. For an instant, Keenan thought it had malfunctioned. Then the rocket motor ignited, spitting blue fire out the back of the missile as the short wings unfolded from the center and tail of the thin fuselage. Now it sailed off, gaining speed.

He jerked the AT4 toward the second launcher, pushed the safety bar forward and jammed his thumb against the red firing button. The AT4 roared. The round, shaped like a thin black turnip with fins, slammed into the second launcher, igniting the fuel in the remaining missile. The launchers and the control room disappeared in a ball of orange fire.

Chan swiveled, tracking the first missile with his AT4. He fired then watched helplessly as the round fell far short of the missile.

"NO!" Keenan screamed again. "God, no!" Both men dropped their empty AT4s and began to fire ineffectively at the swiftly departing missile. Tears ran down Jack Keenan's face as he watched the missile disappear, on its way to incinerate King Shatterhand. That there was only one missile on the way was no consolation.

• • •

The firing had all but stopped outside, but no one had come to announce the FSE's victory over the invaders. A primal feeling swept over Maximov.

"Virograd," the Chairman said, grasping the man's shoulder, "shoot as soon as you are ready! I am going out to supervise the mop-up operation."

The strange scientist looked around at his boss with another unsettling smile.

"We are moments away, Comrade Chairman," he soothed. "We are almost ready."

"I know you will do your duty," Maximov assured Virograd as he slipped out the door of the control room.

"Exactly so," Virograd answered the closing door.

How strange that he did not stay for the launch, Virograd thought. Still it was not necessary and now he would not have to share the joy with anyone.

On the panel in front of him, the last red light turned a welcome green.

"By your command, Comrade Chairman," Virograd said softly.

He flipped up a red switch guard above a label that read ARM. When he threw the small toggle switch, a status light marked WARHEAD ARMED glowed red.

"Now my pet," he cooed, "now you will make the earth shake!" He took a deep breath and pulled the lever that controlled the compressed air.

Virograd's body tensed as the compressed air surged into the launch cannister. A feeling like electricity ran through him as the pressure built for a second and the cannister popped open.

The long bird leaped from the tube, settling into a short fall as its motor ignited. Virograd felt as if his heart would burst from his chest as the flame flickered from the engine and the wings unfolded.

Joy, the joy of unassailable power, swept over him. In a second, he would repeat the process with the second missile. Then his joy would be complete!

Looking down at the console, Virograd did not see the black turnip slam into the side of the remaining missile. He felt the concussion of the explosion and looked up just in time to see the second missile burst into an inferno. He dropped to the floor as the flames and concussion swept over the control center.

He screamed as the fire melted the Plexiglas window and swept into the room.

Kron watched through his binoculars as the last of T'sinko's mortar shells fell on the ground cable car terminal. The place was wrecked.

Another loud boom echoed down from the castle above. On the east wall, an orange flame erupted. Kron smiled. The launchers were destroyed.

His smile turned quickly to a frown as he noticed the thin shape falling away from the castle. He whipped up his binoculars in time to see the missile's engine ignition.

"Fuck our mothers!" he spat, dropping the binoculars and turning around to the motorcycle parked just behind him. He jerked loose the straps holding a long green tube with a box-like arrangement at one end. Lettering on the tube, said: Missile, Anti-aircraft, MANPADS.

He opened the metal case, jerked up the thin missile launcher inside and twisted a short, stubby cylinder into the box below the launch tube.

Muttering imprecations of every sort, Kron flipped up the sight and hefted the contraption to his shoulder. The pale blue missile was passing almost directly overhead now, streaking toward the west.

Kron thumbed down the actuator lever, bringing the Stinger missile's tracking system to life. A second later, the warbling tone in his ear and a buzzing on his cheek confirmed that the infrared seeker had locked onto the SS-NX-21's engine heat.

Kron centered the fleeing missile in the sight, elevated the launcher, pulled the trigger and waited. The missile booster fired, kicking the needle-like missile out of the tube. Its motor ignited half a second later and the Stinger shot off after its prey.

"God guide you," Kron whispered as he watched the tiny missile's plume of white smoke.

"Come on, Jack," Chan urged, "it's gone and we can't stop it!"

"The king," Jack muttered, "he doesn't know it's coming. He . . ."

"He'll have to deal with it," Chan interrupted, "just like we have to deal with these fuckers."

The FSE that had escaped the last firefight were now taking potshots, at them from several directions.

"Jack!" Chan shouted, "Will you snap out of . . ."

A pop from the edge of the village stopped Chan's entreaty. A tiny spark streaked up, following the departing cruise missile.

Keenan grabbed the front of Chan shirt. "Look, Buddha," he shouted. "A Stinger! Look!"

As both men stood staring, the little missile closed the distance to its prey. For an instant, it looked like it would swing wide of the mark, but then it veered in. A large ball of orange fire marked the death of the SS-NX-21. Keenan thought for a second that he could see some debris falling, but what did that matter? England and her king were safe!

"YEEEOOOWW!" Keenan shouted. "Come on, Buddha, what are you waiting for, we need to get off this rock!"

With that, Keenan whirled and fired a short burst from his rifle. A figure tumbled out from behind a pillar.

Behind them, Chan heard a scuffling sound. He jerked his rifle around in time to shove it in Kinski's face.

"Easy, Chan," Mamudi cautioned, running up behind Kinski.

"Where have you two been?" Chan asked.

"Covering your Asian ass," Kinski replied. "What happened here?"

"We got one of the missiles, but the other one launched."

"Oh, shit," Kinski wailed.

"Take it easy," Chan said. "One of the Russians got it with a Stinger from the village!"

"Inshallah!" Mamudi blurted. "It was the will of Allah!"

"I hope he wills us off this rock!" Keenan said, firing at another hidden sniper. "Kinski!" he shouted. "You got us up here. Get us out of here!"

"Buddha," Kinski asked, "where's your glider?"

"Just up there!" Chan answered, pointing to a parapet just above them.

"Is it wrecked?"

"No," Chan answered. "I did it just like you said. It's fine unless some of these FSE creeps got to it."

"Then that's how we'll get out of here!" Kinski said brightly.

"All of us?" the others asked in unison.

"All of us!" Kinski assured them. "Come on." He turned and ran up the ramp that led to the parapet.

"Remind me to check him for a head wound," Mamudi told Chan as the three of them ran after Kinski.

Chan's glider had escaped any damage. It sat unmolested on the narrow parapet, high above the rest of the castle. Kinski leaned over the edge of the battlement. The drop below was dizzying.

"How the hell did you manage to set it down here?" he demanded of Chan.

"Where the hell else was I going to put it?" Chan snapped. "It was either here or right in the middle of a firefight!"

"You did good, Buddha," Kinski smiled. "Now let's get this baby ready to take us out of here!"

"Pete," Keenan interrupted, "will this thing take all of us? I mean, we're no lightweights!"

Kinski stopped and looked at the three others. Their faces did not betray any confidence in his plan.

"Look, guys," he explained, "if we all wanted to soar on this thing, we'd be out of luck. It would never be able to climb carrying this much weight." He pointed over the edge. "But all we want to do is to drop from here to the valley and get there alive." He shook the glider. "This baby will glide us down. It will be a fast ride, but we can make it."

The others still looked skeptical. "If you don't want to do it," Kinski finished, "I'm open to options."

A shot rang out from the courtyard. The bullet buzzed by overhead.

"I don't know if we have any options," Keenan observed.

"Then let's do it!" Chan barked.

Chan's harness lay next to the glider where he had stripped it off. The others were still wearing theirs. They had not had time to remove them in the excitement.

"How are we going to clip in?" Mamudi asked. "There is only one set of clips."

"You and I will be in the middle, both rings in one clip," Kinski improvised. "Buddha and Jack will be on the outsides."

He pulled his combat harness off and stripped out the nylon pistol belt.

"Jack, you and Buddha run the belt through your harness and under your web gear," he instructed. "Loop the belt around the yoke." Mamudi stripped off his belt and gave it to Chan. Keenan threaded Kinski's belt through his harness. Another shot rang out from below.

"Okay," Kinski urged, "let's do it!"

The four men crowded together under the glider. The two lighter men clipped into the glider's suspension. Keenan and Chan, the heavyweights, slipped their web belts through the yoke and then through their harnesses. The four men climbed clumsily up on the parapet. The stiff wind rising up the face of the mountain pulled at the glider, urging it to fly.

"Our Lady of Ballistic Nylon, be with us today," Kinski prayed.

"Do not blaspheme, Peter," Mamudi advised.

"Right," Kinski answered. "Ready? Three, two, one, jump!"

The four men pushed the glider out in front of them and stepped from the parapet. A bullet pinged off the stones as they vanished below the crenellations.

Ernst Kruger was livid with frustration. He had managed to drag himself out in the open, only to find the fight finished. Small groups of FSE troops were milling around below him in the courtyard, but they seemed to have no further interest in the invaders. Many sat clutching their bellies, their heads buried between their legs. Many others lay sprawled where death had overtaken them.

High above him, Kruger could see a flash of black. Crawling toward the edge of the wall he watched the activity above. Suddenly, a man's head appeared above the stone wall. The red hair was all the identification Kruger needed. He sat up, brought up his rifle and fired. The recoil slammed his shoulder into the wall. Pain shot through his chest.

Kruger gritted his teeth, brought the rifle up and fired again. The shot went wide. As he struggled to find a better position, the men high up on the wall suddenly stepped up on the edge of the battlement, holding some huge kite above them. As Kruger watched with amazement, the four disappeared over the side of the Schloss Adler.

• • •

"AAHHHHAAAYYYY," Chan screamed. Next to him, Mamudi, eyes tightly closed, offered up a prayer to Allah.

"OOHHHHH!" Kinski moaned, trying to steer the glider as it swooped to the right. Only Keenan was quiet, watching the valley below with a look of total fascination on his face.

The wind was whistling through the glider's rigging, singing a song as old as aviation itself. To Jack Keenan, it was beautiful music. The green valley below seemed to glow, beckoning them. Directly below them, the cable car terminal burned furiously. The glider swept through the rising smoke. Acrid fumes burned his lungs for one breath, then the sweet cold air returned. Keenan fought to keep his senses intact. All this input was straining his control.

Beside him, Kinski was exhorting the other two Marauders to get a grip and help him steer.

"Damn it, guys," he yelled, "help me out here or we'll all end up on that mountain like four bugs on a bumper!"

Mamudi cut short his prayer and helped Kinski shift the yoke to bring the glider out of its slow right turn. The wind noise continued to increase. The singing now had risen to a siren-like keening. The glider was shaking, but it showed no sign of breaking up.

"God bless Mil Specs!" Keenan laughed. The glider jinked to one side as if it had been jerked on a string. Keenan looked up. There was a deep gouge on one of the wing supports and a ragged hole above the gouge.

As he watched, a red tracer streaked high over the glider. Keenan twisted his head around toward the castle. The glider blocked his view.

"Somebody up there is still pissed," Keenan shouted in Kinski's ear.

Kinski shot Keenan a brief, nervous smile. "Hell, Jack," he shouted, "everyone up there's still pissed!"

It had taken all his strength to pull himself up to the battlement. Kruger leaned as far out as he could, searching the air below the castle for the black glider. It swooped into view, far below and falling fast.

Kruger stuck the rifle out and aimed in front of the speeding dark spec. He fired once, nearly lost his balance and fired again. The red tracer told him he had three more rounds in the magazine. The black glider slipped away, too far below him to see now.

Kruger slumped down and leaned against the stone battlement.

"Bastards!" he spat. "I hope I hit one of them!" He sat there for several minutes, then crawled slowly back toward his room inside the castle.

Kron had been smoking a cigarette and congratulating himself for shooting down the cruise missile when he saw the glider fall off the tallest battlement of the Schloss Adler and plummet toward the valley.

The glider streaked away from the mountain, headed more or less in his direction.

A laugh burst from Kron's throat. "You sons of bitches are still alive!" he yelled. He took one final drag from the cigarette, snuffed it, put the rest in his pocket and straddled the motor bike. Watching the glider swoop down, he kicked the little bike to life and started off after the American madmen.

The green fields below them seemed to rush outward now.

Ground rush, Keenan thought. We'll be down soon. He hoped they would be down in one piece. The glider was screaming across the ground. The bullet hole above him had begun to rip as their speed had increased. Now it was the size of a football.

Ahead of them, a wide field dotted with huge yellow polka dots loomed up. Kinski was obviously steering for the field.

"Haystacks!" Kinski shouted, pointing at the polka dots. The others nodded, each hoping that Kinski's accuracy was up to the task. There would be only one approach.

The ground below was a blur now. The field seemed impossibly far away. Oaths and imprecations of every sort issued from the four men dangling from the black glider as it skimmed over the road and flashed past the edge of the field.

Kinski had managed to line up three of the huge stacks of mown hay. The first stack flashed under them twenty feet below. The second came up fast, looming just ahead.

Keenan's feet caught the top of the stack, flipping them up behind him. The glider skewed to the left from the quick drag, then recovered.

The third haystack suddenly blotted out the sky. With a loud *whump!* the glider and its four petrified passengers slammed into the hay and disappeared from view. Only the glider's wing tips protruded from the big stack.

Kron could see the glider across the open fields. He would not be able to get to it before it landed, but he watched closely to see where it was going so he could find it after it hit. It was in a steep dive, too steep for any safe landing.

As he slid around a turn on the dirt road that led out into the fields, he saw the glider streak by half a mile ahead. It would crash in one of the big open fields. That was lucky. The woods were not far away. A landing there would be fatal, without doubt.

He gunned the bike, throwing a rooster-tail of cold mud behind him as he sped toward the glider's landing field.

He almost drove by it. All that was visible were two black triangles of cloth sticking out of a big haystack.

Kron laughed. The sight was comical, even if deadly serious. Kron gunned the bike, jumped the ditch and plowed through the loose dirt over to the stack.

There was movement below one of the protruding wing tips now. A few seconds later, a dark shape burst through the straw, gasping for breath. Kron recognized the man called Buddha Chan. Behind him, the others emerged, one after the other. In a moment, all four tumbled down from the stack and fell panting onto the cold ground.

"Hello," Kron greeted them, "what were you doing in there?"

"Looking for a needle," Jack Keenan quipped, getting to his feet. "Where's your buddy?"

"He should be on his way back from the village by now," Kron answered. "Are any of you injured?"

"No," Keenan answered. "I don't think so." He turned to the others. "Any of you guys hurt?" Mamudi, slumped back against the stack, raised his hand.

"I'm sorry, Jack," the injured Afghan answered, "it's my ankle. I heard it pop when we hit."

"Come then!" Kron offered. "You can ride back with me!" He looked at Keenan. "Can you find your way back on foot?"

"Bet on it!" Keenan answered as he helped Mamudi over to the motorbike. "We'll beat you there!"

Kron laughed again. "Hang on, my friend!" he told Mamudi over his shoulder, then gunned the bike again and roared off with Mamudi holding on for dear life.

"Come on, guys, saddle up," Keenan goaded the others. "It's Shanks Mare again for us." They struggled to their feet.

"Sorry I didn't get us closer," Kinski apologized.

"Hey, you got us down alive!" Keenan reminded him, as he stripped off the nylon harness and shouldered his rifle. "That was a pretty good trick by itself."

"Yeah, I guess it was!" Kinski said, brightening considerably. He shucked off the harness and dug into his pocket, and pulled out his metal comb. He ran it through his disheveled locks, dragging out a fistful of straw.

"Come on, Pretty Boy," Chan teased him. "Let's hit the road. You can work on your coiffure later!"

With that, the three set off across the open fields. Behind them, oily black smoke still rose from the Schloss Adler and from the ruined cable car terminal below.

The sun was dropping toward the horizon when they ran into T'sinko. He was waiting for them in the forest near the lab. As usual, T'sinko surprised them by stepping out from behind a tree into their path. Only Keenan, with his sixth sense, had any idea the man was there.

"Your friend is all right," T'sinko assured them. "It may only be sprained." He fell in next to them as they walked. "If you wish, we can radio your headquarters and tell them of your success."

Keenan nodded. "That would be good." The conversation lagged for a moment, then T'sinko spoke.

"You did the world a great service, today, *tovarish*," he said quietly. "If you do nothing else, you will be heroes for your actions today!"

"One of you stopped the missile," Keenan observed. "We were too late!"

"That does not matter," T'sinko argued, shaking his head. "You went into the beast's lair and routed him. That is what mattered. Kron only shot down a slow moving missile with an Improved Stinger. That took only skill, not courage."

"Well," Keenan smiled, "you could be right!"

TWENTY-THREE

Yevgeny Maximov was still shaking. The sudden assault, the loss of his missiles and the slaughter of his troops had scared him. The cognac burned his throat and made him cough. A young lieutenant tapped on his open door.

"Comrade Chairman," he reported, "we have located the scientist. He is burned and seems confused, but he is alive."

"Bring him to me," Maximov ordered. "Have you rigged transportation down to the village yet?"

"It is nearly ready, Comrade Chairman," the lieutenant answered. "It will be a frightening ride, I fear."

"That is not your concern, Lieutenant," Maximov barked. "Tell me, where is your Captain?"

"Dead," the young officer replied. "Killed."

"Then you are now a captain," Maximov said. "By tonight, you may be a colonel!"

"Just so, Comrade Chairman," the new captain replied, saluting. "Thank you!"

Maximov waved him away and poured another cognac. No ride could be as frightening as this day had been. He would be thrilled to leave this bird's nest!

The plane landed an hour before dawn on a dirt road ten miles from the weapons lab. As it taxied up to them, Keenan turned to the two Russians.

"We wouldn't be alive except for you two," he said, shaking

their hands. "How do we say thanks for that?"

"By keeping up the fight," Kron answered, "as we will."
T'sinko nodded his agreement.

"Perhaps," the tall officer said, "we may meet again, when
we can drink and enjoy life like normal men!"

"The offer's still good," Keenan shouted over the rising
engine noise.

The Russians shook their heads. "No, my friend," T'sinko
declined, "our place is here. Thank you anyway."

A flurry of handshaking and hearty bearhugs broke out as
the plane lurched to a stop in front of them. A moment later,
the four Americans were aboard and the plane was turning for
its takeoff. The two Spetsnaz waved briefly, then disappeared
into the forest again.

Chan struggled up to the pilot. "Home, James," he shouted
over the engine noise, "and don't spare the horses!" The pilot
laughed and gave him a thumbs-up. The turboprop engine
whined louder and the plane lifted off into the dark sky.

"Well," Chan observed, "I'll bet there'll be a big whing-ding
when we get back! Yes, sir, they'll be dancin' in the streets
when . . ." He stopped his speech when he noticed that his three
companions were all sound asleep.

EPILOGUE

The chairman's orders were very simple. Virograd was to salvage any wreckage that could be found from the missile that had launched, especially the warhead. He was to report if the atomic device was still operable.

The squad that had recovered the downed missile acted like the weapon was radioactive. He had laughed at their officer and called him a fool. The case was still intact. The warhead had not been seriously damaged at all.

"Not as damaged as I was," Virograd murmured. The burns on his back and legs hurt like the devil and his bald head looked grotesque, but he had fared better than many. The invaders had killed dozens of soldiers and officers.

Now, shot up with pain killers, Virograd was back at work. The blue paint on the wrecked missile was scorched black by the explosion. He had instructed the soldiers to place it on the table with the missile access panel up. Under the panel was the computer link.

"We will talk, again, my pretty," Virograd cooed as he unscrewed the four screws that held the plate flush with the missile's skin. He lifted the plate away. Underneath, the computer plug was undamaged.

"Good, good," he cackled. He uncoiled the umbilical cable from the computer console and plugged the fitting into the missile's computer plug.

"Now, my pet," he soothed the missile, "Tell me how you

169

feel." He ran the diagnostics program to check the warhead's status.

The spark of current from the external computer brought the missile's arming microchip back to life. As Virograd watched his monitor, the screen displayed its data. The list of parameters ended with a flashing message that read: Status: DETONATION.

In #9071's dark heart, electrons raced from the capacitor to the detonators buried in the hollow sphere of explosive that surrounded the plutonium core.

Virograd looked up just in time to stare briefly into the blue-white light of eternity.

Then he, the Schloss Adler and the top two thirds of the mountain became one with the cosmos.

IN A WORLD ENSLAVED,
THEY'RE FIGHTING BACK!

Freedom is dead in the year 2030—megacorporations rule with a silicon fist, and the once-proud people of the United States are now little more than citizen-slaves. Only one group of men and women can restore freedom and give America back to the people:

THE NIGHT WHISTLERS

The second American Revolution
is about to begin.

THE NIGHT WHISTLERS #1 by Dan Trevor
Available now from Jove Books!

Here is an exclusive preview . . .

PROLOGUE

Los Angeles, 2030: Seen from afar, the skyline is not all that different from the way it was in earlier decades. True, the Wilshire corridor is stacked with tall buildings, and there are new forms in the downtown complex: the Mitsubishi Towers, a monstrous obelisk in black obsidian; the Bank of Hamburg Center, suggesting a vaguely gothic monolith; the Nippon Plaza with its "Oriental Only" dining room slowly revolving beneath hanging gardens; and, peaking above them all like a needle in the sky, the Trans Global Towers, housing the LAPD and their masters, Trans Global Security Systems, a publicly held corporation.

The most noticeable difference in this city is a silver serpentine arch snaking from downtown to Dodger Stadium and into the Valley, and in other directions—to Santa Monica, to San Bernardino, and to cities in the south. Yes, at long last, the monorail was constructed. The original underground Metro was abandoned soon after completion, the hierarchy claiming it earthquake prone, the historians claiming the power elite did not want an underground system of tunnels where people could not be seen, particularly since the subways in New York and other Eastern cities became hotbeds of resistance for a short period.

But to fully grasp the quality of life in this era, to really understand what it is like to live under the Corporate shadow, one ultimately has to step down from the towers and other heights. One has to go to the streets and join the rank and file.

Those not lucky enough to inherit executive positions usually live in company housing complexes—which are little more than tenements, depending upon the area. The quality of these establishments vary, generally determined by one's position on the corporate ladder. All in all, however, they are grim—pitifully small, with thin walls and cheap appliances and furnishings. There are invariably, however, built-in televisions, most of them featuring seventy-two-inch screens and "Sensound." It is mandatory to view them during certain hours.

When not spouting propaganda, television is filled with mindless entertainment programming and endless streams of commercials exhorting the populace to "Buy! Buy! Buy!" For above all, this is a nation of consumers. Almost all products, poorly made and disposable, have built-in obsolescence. New lines are frequently introduced as "better" and "improved," even though the changes are generally useless and cosmetic. Waste disposal has therefore become one of the major problems and industries of this society. A certain amount of one's Corporate wages is expected to be spent on consumer goods. This is monitored by the Internal Revenue Service and used somewhat as a test of loyalty, an indicator of an individual's willingness to contribute to society.

The Corporations take care of their own on other levels as well. Employees are, of course, offered incentive bonuses, although these are eaten quickly by increased taxes. They are also supplied with recreational facilities, health care, and a host of psychiatric programs, including corporate-sponsored mood drugs. In truth, however, the psychiatric programs are more feared than welcomed, for psychiatry has long given up the twentieth century pretence that it possessed any kind of workable technology to enlighten individuals. Instead, it baldly admits its purpose to bring about "adjustment"—the control and subjugation of individuals "who don't fit in."

Because this is essentially a postindustrial age, and most of the heavy industry has long been shifted abroad to what was once called the Third World, the majority of jobs are basically clerical. There are entire armies of pale-faced word processors, battalions of managers, and legions of attorneys. Entire city blocks are dedicated to data entry facilities, and on any given night, literally thousands of soft-white monitors can be seen glowing through the glass.

There are also, of course, still a few smaller concerns: tawdry bars, gambling dens, cheap hotels, independent though licensed brothels, and the odd shop filled with all the dusty junk that only the poor will buy. And, naturally, there has always been menial labor. Finally there are the elderly and the unemployed, all of whom live in little more than slums.

Although ostensibly anyone may rise through the ranks to an executive position, it is not that simple. As set up, the system invites corruption. Even those who manage to pass the extremely stringent entrance exams and psychiatric tests find it virtually impossible to move up without a final qualifying factor: a sponsor. Unless one is fortunate enough to have friends or relatives in high places, one might as well not even try. If there ever was a classed society, this is it.

In a sense then, the world of 2030 is almost medieval. The Consortium chief executive officers in all the major once-industrial nations rule their regions with as much authority as any feudal lord, and the hordes of clerks are as tied to their keyboards as any serf was ever tied to the land. What were once mounted knights are now Corporate security officers. What was once the omnipotent church is now the psychiatric establishment.

But lest anyone say there is no hope of salvation from this drudgery and entrapment, there are the national lotteries.

Corporately licensed and managed, the Great American Lottery is virtually a national passion. The multitude of ever-changing games are played with all the intensity and fervor of a life-and-death struggle, drawing more than one hundred million participants twice a week. There are systems of play that are as complex and arcane as any cabalistic theorem, and the selection of numbers has been elevated to a religious experience. Not that anyone ever seems to win. At least, not anyone that anyone knows. But at least there is still the dream of complete financial independence and relative freedom.

But if it is an impossible dream that keeps the populace alive, it is a nightmare that keeps them in line. Ever since the Great Upheaval, the Los Angeles Corporate Authority, and its enforcement arm, the LAPD (a Corporate division) have kept this city in an iron grip. And although the LAPD motto is still

"To Protect and Serve," its master has changed and its methods are as brutal as those of any secret police. It is much the same in all cities, with all enforcement agencies around the world under the authority of Trans Global.

What with little or no legal restraint, suspects are routinely executed on the streets, or taken to the interrogation centers and tortured to or past the brink of insanity. Corporate spies are everywhere. Dissent is not tolerated.

And yet, in spite of the apparently feudal structure, it must be remembered that this is a high-tech world, one of laser-enhanced surveillance vehicles, sensitive listening devices, spectral imaging weapon systems, ultrasonic crowd control instruments, and voice-activated firing mechanisms.

Thus, even if one were inclined to create a little havoc with, for instance, a late-twentieth-century assault rifle, the disparity is simply too great. Yes, the Uzi may once have been a formidable weapon, but it is nothing compared to a Panasonic mini-missile rounding the corner to hone in on your pounding heartbeat.

Still, despite the suppression, despite the enormous disparity of firepower, despite the odds, there are still a few—literally a handful—who are compelled to resist. This savage world of financial totalitarianism has not subdued them. Rather, if it has taught them anything at all, it is that freedom can only be bought with will and courage and blood.

This is the lesson they are trying to bring to the American people, this and an ancient dream that has always stirred the hearts of men.

The dream of freedom.

ONE

The city was still sleeping when the whistling began. The streets were still deserted, and the night winds still rattled through strewn garbage. Now and again, from deep within the tenement bowels came reverberations of harsh shouts, the slamming of a loosely hinged door. But otherwise there was nothing beyond the echo of that solitary whistler.

For a full thirty seconds Phillip Wimple stood stock-still and listened, the collar of his sad and shapeless raincoat turned up against the foul wind. He looked out at the city with calm brown eyes, his slightly lined face expressionless. He stood as detectives the world over stand, with all the weight on his heels, hands jammed into the pockets of his trousers, his cropped, gray head slightly cocked to the left.

Although not a particularly reflective man, those high nocturnal melodies had always left Wimple vaguely pensive. As to the fragment of some half-remembered tune that continually tugs at one's memory, he had always felt compelled to listen—to turn his tired eyes to the grimy Los Angeles skyline and allow the sounds to enter him.

A patrolman approached, a sleek doberman of a man in Hitachi body armor and a Remco mini-gun harness. Below, on a stretch of filthy pavement that skirted the weed-grown hill, stood four more uniformed patrolmen. Gillette M-90s rested on their hips. The darkened visors of crash helmets concealed their eyes. Turbo-charged Marauders idled softly beside them in the blackness.

"With all due respect, sir, the Chief Inspector wants to know what's holding us up."

Wimple turned again, shifting his gaze to the distant outline of an angular face behind a smoked Marauder windshield. "Well, tell her that if she would be so kind as to join me on this vantage point, I would be more than happy to explain the delay."

"Sir?"

"Ask Miss Strom to come up here."

Wimple returned his gaze to the skyline. Although the whistling had grown fainter, scattered by the predawn breeze, the melody was still audible: high and cold above the city's haze; dark and threatening in the pit of his stomach.

The woman entered his field of vision, an undeniably grim figure in black spandex and vinyl boots—a full-figured woman, about an inch taller than his five-ten. Her shimmering windbreaker was emblazoned with the Corporate logo: twin lightning bolts enclosed in a fist. When Wimple had first laid on eyes on her, he took her as a welcome change from the usual Corporate overlord. Not only was she smart, but she was beautiful . . . in a carnivorous way. He had also liked her fire, her determination, and her willingness to fight for a budget. But that was three days ago. Now, watching her stiffly approach through the smog-choked weeds and yellowed litter, he realized that Miss Erica Strom was no different from any of the boardroom commandants sent down to ensure that the Los Angeles Police Department toed the Corporate line.

"You want to tell me what's going on?" Miss Strom planted herself beside him.

Wimple shrugged, studying her profile: the chiseled features, the red-slashed lips, the hair like a black lacquered helmet. "Ever heard a rattler's hiss?" he asked.

Strom narrowed her sea-green eyes at him. "What are you talking about?"

Wimple extended his finger to the sky to indicate the echo of the unseen whistlers. "That," he said. "That sound."

Withdrawing a smokeless cigarette, one of the Surgeon General–sanctioned brands that tasted like wet hay, Wimple said, "Think of it like this. We're the cavalry. They're the Indians.

Maybe they can't touch us up here, but down there it's a whole different story."

"So what are you trying to tell me? That you want to call this patrol off? You want to turn around and go to bed, because some Devo starts whistling in the dark?" Her deep voice had a masculine edge, a hardness.

Wimple shook his head with a tired smirk. Devo: Corporate catchword for any socially deviate individual, generally from the menial work force. "No, Miss Strom," he said, "I'm not trying to tell you that I want to call the patrol off. I'm just saying that if we go down there now, we could find ourselves in one hell of a shit storm."

Strom returned the detective's smirk. "Is that so?"

"Yes, ma'am."

"Well, in that case, Detective, move your men on down. I can hardly wait."

Long favored by patrolmen throughout the Greater Los Angeles sprawl, the Nissan-Pontiac Marauder was a formidable machine. With a nine-liter, methane-charged power plant, the vehicle was capable of running down virtually anything on the road, and was virtually unstoppable by anything less than an armor-piercing shell. Long and low, it was not, however, built for comfort, and the off-road shocks always wreaked havoc on Wimple's spine.

He rode shotgun beside Miss Strom: shoulders hard against the polymer seats, feet braced on the floorboards, right hand firm on the sissy bar. Earlier, when Strom had given the order to move out, there had been several whispered complaints from the patrolmen. Now, however, as the three-vehicle convoy descended into the black heart of the city, the radios were silent.

"Why don't you tell me about them?" Miss Strom said, easing the Marauder onto the wastes of First Street.

Wimple shrugged, his eyes scanning the tenement windows above. "There's not really much to tell," he replied. "About eighteen months ago, we start getting reports of a little Devo action from the outlying precincts. Vandalism mostly. Petty stuff. Then come July and one of the IRS stations goes up in smoke. After that, we start finding it spray-painted all over the walls: Night Whistlers."

"Any idea who's behind it?"

"Yeah, we've got some ideas."

Strom's thin lips hardened. "So what's been the problem? Why haven't you cleaned them out yet?"

Wimple lifted his gaze to the long blocks of tenements ahead—to the smashed windows and rotting doorways, the grimy, crumbling brickwork and trashed streets. "Well, let's just say that the Whistlers turned out to be a little more organized than we thought." His voice was dull, noncommittal. She gave him a quick look then went back to scanning the street.

They had entered the lower reaches of Ninth Street, and another long canyon of smog-browned tenements. For the most part, the residents here were members of the semiskilled labor force, popularly known as the Menials, officially referred to in ethnological surveys as the Lower Middle Class. Included among their ranks were whole armies of word processors, retail clerks, delivery boys, receptionists, and secretaries. By and large, their lives were measured out in pitiful production bonuses, worthless stock options, and department store clearance sales. They also, of course, spent a lot time pouring over their lottery tickets, and even more in front of their television screens, watching tedious Corporate-controlled programming. Still, no matter how blatant the propaganda, it was more entertaining than their dull existences.

The radio came alive with a harsh metallic burst from the last Marauder in the line: "Possible six-twenty on Hill."

Six-twenty meant curfew violation—which invariably meant Devo action.

Strom dropped her left hand from the steering wheel and activated the dispatch button on the dashboard. "Let's show them a response now, gentlemen." Then bringing the Marauder into a tight turn, she activated the spectral-imaging screen and switched the infrared cameras to the scan mode.

Wimple, however, preferred to use his eyes. He initially saw only a half-glimpsed vision among the heaps of uncollected refuse: a thin, brown figure in a drab-green duffle coat. For a moment, a single perverse moment, he actually considered saying nothing. He actually considered returning his gaze to the bleak stretch of road ahead, casually withdrawing another smokeless cigarette and keeping his mouth firmly shut. But even as this thought passed through his mind, the image of the fleeing figure appeared on the screen.

The radio crackled to life again with a voice from the second Marauder. "I've got clean visual."

There was a quick glimpse of a sprinting form beneath a sagging balcony, the sudden clamor of a trash can on the pavement.

Strom powered her vehicle into another hard turn, screeching full-throttle into the adjoining alley. Then as she deftly lowered her thumb to activate the spotlight, he was suddenly there: a wiry Hispanic huddled beneath an ancient fire escape.

Strom activated the megaphone, and her voice boomed out in harsh, clipped syllables: "Remain where you are! Any attempt to flee will be met with force!"

The figure stumbled back to the alley wall, glaring around like a blinded bull. He was younger than Wimple had first imagined, no more than ten or twelve. His duffle coat was army surplus. His blue jeans were Levi knockoffs. He also wore a pair of black market running shoes—the badge of the Devos.

Strom eased the Marauder to a stop alongside the number two and three vehicles. Then, reaching for the stun gun beneath the dash, she slipped free of her harness and turned to Wimple. "Come on, Detective, let me show you what law and order is all about."

Strom and Wimple approached the suspect slowly. To their left and right, scanning the rooftops with Nikon-Dow Night Vision Systems atop their M-90s, were the four helmeted patrolmen from the backup Marauders. Given the word, they would have been able to pour out some six hundred fragmentation flechettes in less than a fifty-second burst—more than enough to shred the kneeling suspect to a bloody pulp.

Wimple looked at the boy's scared eyes. They kept returning to the stun-gun that dangled from Strom's gloved hand.

Manufactured for Trans Global by Krause-Nova Electronics in Orange County, the XR50 Stun gun had become the last word on hand-held crowd control. It was capable of dispersing a scatter charge of nearly fifty-thousand volts, instantly immobilizing a two-hundred-pound man. At closer range, and against bare skin, the pain was beyond description.

The boy could not keep himself from shivering when Strom laid the cold tip of the stun gun against his cheek, could not

keep himself from mouthing a silent plea. In response, however, Strom merely smiled, and turned to Wimple again.

"Why don't you see what he's carrying, Detective? Hmm?
See what our little lost lamb has in his pockets."

Wimple pressed the boy facedown to the pavement, con-
sciously avoiding the terrified eyes. He then lowered himself
to a knee and mechanically began the search. On the first pass,
he withdrew only a greasy deck of playing cards, a half-eaten
chocolate bar, and a stainless steel identity tag made out to
one Julio Cadiz. Then, almost regretfully, he slowly peeled a
six-inch steak knife from the boy's left ankle.

"Well, well, well." Strom smiled. "What have we here?"

Wimple rose to his feet, turning the steak knife over in his
fingers. "These things don't necessarily mean much."

Strom let her smile sag into another smirk. "Is that so, Detective?"

"It's just kind of a status symbol with these kids. They don't
ever really use them. They just like to carry them around to
show off to their buddies."

But by this point, Strom had already withdrawn a pair of
keyless handcuffs . . . had already released the safety on the
stun-gun.

She secured the boy's wrists behind his back, then yanked
up his coat and T-shirt to expose the base of the spine. Although
once or twice the boy emitted a pleading whimper, he still hadn't
actually spoken.

"Tell your men to secure the area," Strom said as she
hunkered down on the pavement beside the handcuffed boy.
Then again when Wimple failed to respond: "Secure the area,
Detective. Tell your men."

Wimple glanced over his shoulder to the blank faces of
the patrolmen. Before he actually gave the order, however,
he turned to the woman again. "Look, I'm not trying to tell
you how to do your job, Miss Strom, but this is not going to
get us anywhere. You understand what I'm saying? And this
is not a safe place for us to be wasting our time."

Strom ran a contemplative hand along the gleaming shaft of
the stun-gun, then dropped her gaze to the shivering boy. Not
looking at Wimple, she finally said, "Detective, I think you
should get your men to secure the area before this little brat
starts screaming and brings out the whole neighborhood."

She waited until the patrolmen posted on the corner fixed their night vision systems on the balconies and rooftops and chambered clips of flechettes into their weapons. Then very gently, very slowly, she pressed the cold tip of the stun gun to the boy's naked spine.

"Look—," Wimple began.

"Shut up, Detective," she said, her eyes cold, then lowered her gaze back to the boy.

"Well, now, young man. You and I are going to have a little heart to heart. You understand? A frank exchange of views, with you starting first."

An involuntary shudder crossed the thin, feral face of the boy. "Look, lady, I don't know—"

She clamped her hand to his mouth. "No, no, no. That's not how this game is played, my little friend. In this game, you don't speak until I ask a question. Got it?"

The boy may have tried to nod, but Strom had taken hold of his hair. Then, yanking back his head so that his ear was only inches from her lips, she whispered, "Whistlers, my little man. How about telling me what you know about the Whistlers?"

The boy responded with another frenzied shiver, then possibly attempted to mouth some sort of response. But by this time Strom had released his head, activated the stun gun, and pressed the tip home.

The boy seemed to react in definite stages to the voltage, first arching up like a quivering fish, then growing wide-eyed and ridged as the scream tore out of his body. And even when it stopped, he still seemed to have difficulty breathing, while the left leg continued to tremble.

"Now, let's try it again, shall we?" Strom cooed. "Who . . . are . . . the Whistlers?"

The boy shook his head before answering in spluttering gasps. "Look, lady, I don't know what you're talking about. I swear to God. The Whistlers, that's just something that they write on the walls."

"Who writes it on the walls?"

"I don't know. Just some of the Devos around here. I don't know who they are."

"Just some of the Devos, huh? Well, I'm sorry, young man, but that's just not good enough." And lifting up his T-shirt again to expose the base of his spine, she laid down another fifty-thousand volts.

There was something horrifying about the way the boy's eyes grew impossibly wide as he thrashed on the pavement with another trailing scream. There was also something chilling about the way Strom's lips twisted up in a smile as she watched.

Wimple turned his head away, stared for a moment into some distant blackness. Finally, unable to stand the sobs any longer, he approached again.

"Look, don't you think that's enough, Miss Strom? *Miss Strom!*"

She slowly turned on her haunches to face him, her left hand still toying with the boy's sweat-drenched hair. "You got a problem, Detective?"

Wimple met her gaze for a full three seconds before answering, a full three seconds to taste the woman's hatred. "Yeah," he finally nodded. "I got a problem. Quite apart from my personal objection to this activity, I'd like to point out that you are seriously endangering my men. If you think that this neighborhood is asleep right now, you are sadly mistaken. The people up in those buildings know exactly what's going on down here. They know exactly what you're doing, and I can assure you that they don't like it."

She withdrew her fingers from the boy's hair, and his head lolled back to the vomit-smeared pavement. "Well, now, that's very interesting, Detective. Because, you see, I *want* them to know what's going on here. I *want* them to hear every decibel of this little bastard's scream, and, remember it—"

"Shut up!"

"How dare you tell me to—"

"Shut up and listen!" Wimple said, as the first cold notes of the solitary whistler wafted down from the blackened rooftops.